MELODY IN
HER
Heart

BOOK 1

 HEALING HEARTS
A *Lesbian Medical Romance* Drama Series

MT CASSEN

CHAPTER ONE

Tabby

The scent of lavender drifted through the halls of the emergency room as Tabitha Brickly exited one of her patient's rooms. Lavender, for its calming effect. Tonight, it provided tranquility more than it did previous nights. She heaved a sigh, taking in the whiff that was briefly intermixed with the smell of coffee. As nurses, they all thrived on coffee—some more than others—and Tabby caught herself needing a massive caffeine kick at that very moment.

Tabby grabbed a carafe and poured herself half a cup. She only had fifteen minutes left, then she would be out of there. Sometimes, the minutes seemed to tick by, taking way too long to finalize the night. She checked her watch as she sunk into a chair at the nurses' station.

Tabby took a sip of coffee, then reached for her phone. After dialing her home phone, she waited as the line rang three times. Tabby tapped her foot along to the sound of each ring. *Answer the phone, someone.*

She was just about to hang up when someone picked up. "Hello?" Brittany, her eldest daughter, said.

"Hey, Britt. How are you doing? I didn't think anyone was home."

"Dad was playing his music so loud," her daughter replied, her voice a near-groan. "Are you coming home? We're starving!"

Tabby forced a smile. Her life was left to working, cooking, cleaning, and anything that wasn't a leisurely activity. Usually, she didn't let that bother her, but the starving comment struck her at that moment. After working twelve hours in the ER, all she wanted to do was crash, not think of what to have for supper. Still, as a wife and a mother, she knew it was impossible to stand her ground all the time. But this one time left her wanting to tell her family they should fix something themselves.

"I'll be home in half an hour. What sounds good? Pizza?" It was an easy thing to make—toss it in the oven, and you're done. The groan on the other end wasn't promising.

"We just had pizza," Brittany argued. "Remember?"

"I'll figure something out," Tabby said, stifling a yawn as she took a sip of her coffee.

"Tabby! Emergency coming in!" She looked up to see Hanna rushing past her. Tabby quickly stood up.

"I'll see you all in a bit," she said. "Gotta run."

"Bye, Mom," Brittany said, and Tabby disconnected the call.

As she hurried to the doors where the nurses had all gathered, Tabby knew it was less likely that she would be out of there in ten minutes. She couldn't think about that, as it would only be another disappointment to her two children. Brittany, who was thirteen, might be more apt to understand. But Callie —she was only nine. Seeing the disappointment in her younger daughter's eyes was always hard to swallow. It wasn't like they were home alone, though. Drew was there and able to manage just fine, but Tabby only hoped that he would step up to the plate and take over certain responsibilities, as their father should do.

The doors opened, and two EMTs came rushing in with one gurney. "Multiple vehicle accident," the one woman said. "There's more to come."

The few nurses there went to work as the gurneys came through the door one by one. Tabby went along with one of them, pushing a woman into one of the vacant rooms.

"Jane Doe," an EMT started. "Eighteen to twenty years old. Crushed legs in the crash as she was thrown from her vehicle and another vehicle landed on her lower extremities."

"Has she gained consciousness yet?" Tabby asked, leaning over her as she started to cut her clothes off. They waited for the ER doctor to take care of her case.

"For about ten minutes, a witness states. Lost a lot of blood."

"Thanks," Tabby said grimly as Dr. Maxwell entered the room.

"What do we have for IV access?" Dr. Maxwell said in a cool and professional voice.

The EMT replied, "We have two 18-gauge IVs running lactated ringers wide open."

"Someone had better call blood bank," Dr. Maxwell said. "We'll need four units of O-negative packed red cells, fresh frozen plasma, and platelets—STAT." He pulled a stethoscope from his lab coat and listened intently to the patient's chest. "Where's the radiology tech?"

One of the ER nurses replied, "He's rounding the corner with the mobile X-ray machine."

"Good," Dr. Maxwell said. "We'll need a head-to-toe bone series."

Behind Dr. Maxwell was a flurry of activity as nurses placed orders for labs, X-rays, and CT scans. Tabby ran the vitals as Dr. Maxwell conducted an exam and Sally, another nurse, worked on preparing the patient's legs to be checked. Once the patient was stabilized, she was ready to be wheeled off to her first CT scan.

Tabby hurried through the hallway with Sally at the other end of the gurney, and they pushed her into the radiology suite across from the emergency department. "I thought you were in the nursery tonight. I haven't seen you all night."

"We're having a slow night, and we heard there was an emergency coming in. Gotta go where you're needed."

"Absolutely. How are the other patients?" she asked. "Have you seen?"

"Two deceased that I know of," Sally said. She shook her head. "Life can be so unfair, don't you think?"

Tabby nodded. "It can be cruel. That's for sure."

They passed the radiology desk and entered the chilly room housing the CT scanner. The CT techs were already waiting for them and carefully transferred the patient to the scanner's movable table. Tabby leaned against the wall and stared down at her watch as Sally propped herself against the wall across from her.

"You're going to be getting out late, aren't you?" she asked.

Tabby sighed. "Can't be helped. It's the life of a nurse."

"Love it or leave it, and we all love it too much, so how could we leave it?" Sally smiled as she spoke the words.

Sally was right. Tabby loved working as a nurse. Even though she had gotten into the profession thinking it was a way to help her growing family, she had found that it was a way to serve the community and feel the difference she was making to the world. She never once regretted her decision.

While she worked in the emergency room part-time, her main focus was the cardiology ward. Going into the field, she had assumed she would thrive best with pediatrics. Quickly, she had learned that she couldn't stomach seeing a child in pain. It was even harder when it was one of her own, but she couldn't keep working in pediatrics when her heart ached for those kids. Cardiology seemed to be a good fit. When they needed fill-ins, she was there to help out. They appreciated that despite Tabby having a family, she still found time to lend a hand when they needed it. It didn't always please her family, but even they understood the importance she brought to Capmed. She just hoped they weren't upset with her that she had broken one more promise.

The lights were only lit in the kitchen as Tabby drew closer to the driveway. She heaved a sigh and parked her car. She could picture Drew already asleep. The clock on the radio ran a few minutes late, but it was nearing nine o'clock, and that was two hours longer than she expected it to be.

"It's my job," Tabby rehearsed, heading up to the front door. "I couldn't just leave."

She didn't even know the purpose of rattling off her pleas for him to forgive her for missing the children's supper. It wasn't like it was anything new, and if he wanted to be crabby when she first saw him, then nothing she said would change that.

Tabby stepped into the foyer. The silence was the first thing that hit her. The glow remained from the kitchen and down the hallway. She dropped her purse and headed toward the light. When she rounded the corner, she saw Drew sitting at the kitchen table, his back to her.

"Are the kids in bed?" Tabby asked.

He looked over his shoulder, then shook his head and stood. "Hello to you, too," he huffed. "Do you know what time it is? Of course they're in bed. They have school tomorrow. You would have been angry if they weren't." He paused beside her. "Don't worry; I fed them a peanut butter sandwich. They're fine."

"Do you want something to eat? I can whip you up something in less than fifteen minutes." Tabby rushed over to the counter and started pulling things from the cupboard. She wasn't sure what she was going to cook, but she would make something work.

"Don't bother," he mumbled. "Not hungry."

He left the kitchen, leaving Tabby alone. She stared down at the pots and pans on the counter and immediately started putting them away. There was a knot in the pit of her stomach. It wasn't different from any other night. She spent many nights in the kitchen, alone, just eating by herself. Yet she always expected things to get better. But why?

Tabby opened the cupboard and pulled out a box of cereal. In two minutes, she would have dinner and pretend like she was having steak or some other fancy feast that someone else prepared for her. Drew's music started as she took her first bite.

Drew was a good father, where it mattered. He didn't abuse the children, he loved them, and he was around, mostly. That was mainly because he had nowhere else to be. Clients weren't exactly beating down his door, hoping he'd provide musical services for them. It wasn't surprising since Tabby rarely saw him out there trying to get gigs. I have to hone my skills, Tab. You're not a musician; you just wouldn't understand. If she had a nickel for every time he gave her that line, she would surely be rich, and he wouldn't need to work. As it stood, she provided all the income anyway. And it was precisely why she stayed all the extra hours she could. Did she want to stay away from her daughters for that long? No!

These were their impressionable years, the years her children should look back and not have to say that things were messed up for them. Tabby hoped she wouldn't hear them one day say they regretted the time she spent away from them. She was doing this *for* them. That was the one line she had to tell herself repeatedly.

She took a bite of her cereal and cringed as Drew hit a shaky note. The note was clearly out of tune, and if she knew him well, she knew that any minute, he'd come storming into the kitchen, complaining that he needed some new strings.

She rolled her eyes at the sound of incoming footsteps. *Just like clockwork.*

"Stupid strings," Drew muttered. "I know I have some new ones in here somewhere." He pulled out a junk drawer and tossed it on the table, then started to leaf through it like he was a madman looking for some buried treasure.

"Are you sure they aren't in the room?" Tabby asked. "I feel like—"

"What are you yammering about?" he asked, turning to look at Tabby.

She dropped her eyes to the mess he had already made on the kitchen table. "Your guitar strings…" She looked up and met his gaze. "I feel like they're on the top of the dresser in the bedroom."

He huffed and turned away from her. "I would remember if they were," he said. "I haven't seen them in several days." He went back to rummaging, then flipped the drawer over, emptying the contents on the top of the kitchen table.

Tabby's eyes fell to the mess that had only gotten bigger. Drew mumbled something incoherent and stormed out of the kitchen, leaving the mess behind. Tabby shook her head and took another spoonful of her cereal. She wanted to ignore the mess, just like he had. It wasn't her style, though. After she finished her food, she washed her bowl and spoon and put them back in their correct places, then turned to the mess that Drew had left behind for her to clean up.

His footsteps sounded, coming back down the steps, but Tabby didn't stop. She soon had everything back in the drawer, which she put away before turning the light off and leaving the kitchen. When she hit the hallway, the music sounded again. She stopped in the living room.

"Find the strings?" she asked.

"Yeah," he mumbled, never looking up from his guitar. She would never say I told you so, because that wouldn't get her anywhere.

"All right then. I'm going to head on up to bed. Are you coming?"

"I've got too much work to do. Goodnight." Again, his eyes stayed on his music.

"Goodnight," she mumbled before leaving the living room and going up the stairs to peek in on the girls. Drew just sometimes didn't realize the way he cut across, especially when it came to being around Tabby. There were times when she thought hard about what it would mean to walk away from their marriage, but that was never an easy decision. For her, it came down to the girls. She didn't want to uproot their lives; it wasn't fair to them. But it also wasn't fair for her to stay if she wasn't happy.

She stopped at Callie's room and peeked her head inside to see her daughter sleeping soundly. Callie's light was on, next to her bed, and her glasses were still propped on her nose. Tabby entered the room and reached to take her glasses off.

"Mom?" Callie whispered groggily.

"Shh," Tabby replied, kneeling next to her. "I'm sorry I wasn't home."

"It's okay," she said. "You were taking care of people."

Tabby smiled, brushing her hand along Callie's forehead. "That's right, honey." She leaned in and kissed her forehead. "Go back to sleep."

"Goodnight, Mom," Callie whispered before rolling onto her side.

Tabby could see Callie being the daughter that would want to live with Tabby for the rest of her life. She was a momma's girl, and Tabby loved that about her sweet little girl, even if it wasn't realistic. She turned her lamp off and then left the room, giving her one last look before stepping into the hallway and closing the door behind her. It was a relief that Callie wasn't upset, as Tabby thought she would be. Now on to Brittany to see if she had to smooth things over with her.

She reached Brittany's room, noticing the door was ajar. She carefully pushed the door open and looked at the bed. Brittany had a book propped on her legs, with her book light attached. Tabby cleared her throat, and Brittany jerked to attention. Even in the dark room, Tabby noticed her daughter's cheeks turning red.

"Hey, Mom!" She closed her book and put it off to the side. "I was just about to go to bed."

"You should have been in bed nearly an hour ago." Tabby sat down on the chair that rested against Brittany's bed. Brittany gave a sheepish grin.

"I couldn't sleep knowing you were out there. I had to wait up." She batted her eyelashes, and Tabby smiled gently. Out of her two children, Brittany was the one with the big imagination. She was thirteen going on thirty and had a mind of her own. Thus far, it worked in her favor, so Tabby felt no need to discipline her for staying up past her bedtime. She was a straight A student and would get up in plenty of time to meet the bus, probably an hour before she needed to.

"Now that you see I'm here, you'd best get some rest for

those pretty blue eyes of yours." Tabby kissed her forehead. "Sweet dreams."

"Night, Mom." Brittany turned off her book light, and Tabby walked over to the door.

"Goodnight." She gave her daughter one long look and then left her room.

Brittany was Tabby's world. When Tabby found out she was pregnant at seventeen, she feared that everyone would say she had to get rid of her. In an instant, the baby growing inside of her had become her life. Yet she had worried that she wouldn't be able to be the parent that she always wanted to be. Her parents were a great example for Tabby, and she wanted a family like that.

There was a time, though, during the first months of her pregnancy when she had considered raising Brittany alone. How different might her life if she had? Days like today when she struggled to have a simple conversation with Drew seriously made her wonder.

Her family and Drew had all pushed her into marriage. While she had wanted to get married before Brittany was born, Brittany had other ideas. She had come a month early into the world, derailing most of their plans. For years, they had the perfect family, until slowly, things started to fade. The honeymoon phase started to wane. Then came Callie. After she was born, their marriage got better. They had gotten married too young, and marriage counseling had been key in helping them learn how to compromise and grow in their love because they had lost sight of that somewhere along the way. But now things were only growing darker for them as a couple and a family.

Tabby stepped into the bedroom and looked over at the empty bed. There used to be a time when Drew would never want her to go to bed alone. She couldn't even remember the last time they made love. Her nights had become lonely. How much more of that could she take? Something needed to change, or there was no way this could last, kids or not.

CHAPTER TWO

Jenni

Traffic was a nightmare. Horns blaring at people going too slowly on the freeway, a crash that caused one off-ramp to shut down completely, and people just trying to get to their destination safely. Jennifer just wanted to get to her board meeting.

Her car inched up one more spot, then came to another complete halt. "Come on!" she yelled at her front window, staring at the line of traffic in front of her. Her day was already one fiasco after another. From waking up late to rushing to shower and get out the door, only allotting time for one cup of coffee, she had figured the day would be a bust. Then, as she had gotten into her car, her blouse had torn at the seam, and it was back in the house to find something else to wear.

When she got on the freeway, she had assumed it would be

a smooth ride. She hadn't accounted for the traffic that would be out in full force. Jenni looked down at her clock radio. If she could barrel through traffic and not have to worry about stopping for even one second, she would only be five minutes late.

She groaned and tapped on the steering wheel. There wasn't any chance of that happening, so she just needed to try to calm down. A person whizzed out from around her, honking their horn as they zoomed by, and Jenni looked out at the traffic in front of her. "Why didn't I think of that?"

She quickly skirted out around the cars and pressed her foot on the gas, going ten over the speed limit. For the first time since getting on the freeway, she was able to get some momentum going. "Finally!" she muttered. As long as there was a break in traffic for her to pass other cars, she would be able to get off the ramp and make it to Capmed before they sent out the search dogs.

When a siren sounded, Jenni glanced in her rearview mirror, her eyes dropping as she clutched her steering wheel. Just one more thing to keep her from getting to her destination. She maneuvered her vehicle to the side of the road, fuming over the fact that she was the only one to be pulled over.

"License and registration," the officer said in greeting. She leaned over and whipped it out of her glove box, wanting to explain to him that it wasn't her idea to cut around everyone like that. She was only following the other driver's lead. She didn't think the officer would take too kindly to that, though. Jenni stared straight ahead, anxious for him to just give her a ticket and let her on her way.

Twenty minutes later, she turned into the parking lot of Capmed with a ticket and a hefty fine pinned to her visor. Such was her day. Maybe if she had time for more than one cup of coffee, she would have wound up with a better morning. Thus far, the day didn't seem to be on her side.

Jenni hurried from the car with her purse over her shoulder, which hit her as she jogged to the ER entrance. They couldn't start the board meeting without her, which was all the more reason to try to get there before too much time had been lost.

She stepped over a root that came up through the ground, and her ankle twisted, accompanied by a snapping sound. Jenni froze. "You have got to be kidding me." She reached down and pulled her shoe off, staring at the broken heel in front of her. Mark it up to one more rotten notch on her day. She could only be thankful for one thing, that she hadn't gone flying face-first to the ground. Don't even consider that, or it'll happen next.

Jenni reached down and pulled off her other shoe, then carried them both in one hand as she ran through the parking lot. It would beat the hobbling she would be forced to do if she kept only one heel to the ground. Who cared if she looked like a madwoman, running toward the hospital, bare feet kicking up dust along the way?

As she approached the curb along the parking lot, a woman with a young son and daughter in tow approached. The little girl giggled and pointed at Jenni's bare feet.

"Mommy, look," the girl said.

The mother nodded and smiled sympathetically at Jenni, understanding passing between them. Broken heels were something most women could relate to. Jenni waved at the little girl as the family of three walked away. Jenni paused, watching them as they located their car. Her heart ached, a pang of longing strong in her chest. She had always wanted to be a mother and had dreamed of it most of her life. But sometimes life didn't go as planned. Jenni doubted she could even conceive anymore, at her age.

She had hope once. She had a wife. And after months of trying, they were close to finally conceiving. But then she had lost everything in an instant...

Brushing the thought aside because it wouldn't get her anywhere, she turned, speed walking toward the ER entrance. As she passed through the sliding glass doors, another woman simultaneously came up to the door. They collided, making Jenni bounce back in shock. "Wow, guess I need glasses," Jenni said jokingly.

The woman turned and looked at her. "It was me. I wasn't paying any attention. Sorry," she mumbled.

Jenni took a moment to recover, caught off guard by the woman's dazzling blue eyes. Her blonde hair cascaded around her shoulders, and a barrette pulled back her bangs. Her hair was shiny, perhaps freshly highlighted. The woman had smiled when they made eye contact, but it didn't reach her eyes. If anything, Jenni thought she saw tears. Like maybe she had been crying the morning away and only just stopped. The woman's eyes were slightly red, and with her lack of makeup, they didn't go unnoticed. At least, not to Jenni. Her eyes were beautiful but distant, and her nose was small and slightly upturned. Her face lacked wrinkles, the kind that came with old age. She had a youthful impression about her, even though she looked like she was in her early thirties.

Jenni had the urge to reach out and hug her, to tell her everything would be okay. She knew what it was like to hurt, and she only wanted to help this beautiful woman with her pain.

The woman's lips curved into another forced smile, and Jenni caught herself returning the gesture. Jenni realized she had been staring heavily, the board meeting forgotten. She pushed her hair behind her ear and quickly looked away. Next to this woman, Jenni felt like an old hag, trying to imitate someone who still had life in her.

"No harm. I wasn't injured or anything." Jenni laughed, hoping she would see the woman smile again. Mission accomplished.

Jenni caught herself breathlessly, releasing another laugh. Calm down, Jenni. Your heart is racing, and you're liable to make a fool of yourself. Although Jenni was pretty sure she had already achieved that. All that gawking had to be making things a bit awkward.

"So, um, yeah…. I should get going," Jenni said.

"Yeah, me too." The woman's eyes dipped to Jenni's shoes, and she frowned.

"Long story," Jenni mumbled. "Such is my day. And with that note…" She started to push past her, and her eyes moved to the woman's left hand. There was a wedding band on her ring finger. It wasn't the least bit surprising, because the woman was magnetizing, but a pang of regret hit Jenni in the chest. She probably also had a house full of kids. She continued past her. "Nice to bump into you." She smirked. "Literally."

"Same," the woman said. As Jenni rushed past her and to the elevator, where the door was just closing, she felt the woman's eyes on her. Perhaps it was her imagination. Yet, when she turned around, she met the woman's gaze. Jenni smiled and waved, and the door closed. She wasn't wrong. The woman seemed distracted by her, though it was likely only because Jenni looked a chaotic mess. She shook her head and fell back against the wall of the elevator. The woman was dressed in scrubs, so she was obviously an employee there. But where? What department? She didn't recall any interactions with her before, and they surely wouldn't have gone unnoticed. She would have remembered that face and those eyes.

What unsettled Jenni the most, though, was how the woman sparked something in her that reminded her of the spark she originally had with her wife, Wendy. She missed Wendy and still found it hard to think of her. She also missed companionship and someone to come home to. She filled her life with work because it distracted her from the loneliness and fading memories.

She heaved a sigh and shook her head. It was best to just forget about the strange woman. Longing for something she could never have—kids and a loving wife—would only create stress. She was too old to conceive, and moving on without Wendy would fill her with too much guilt. She needed to focus on work because there was a lot at stake.

The doors opened, and she straightened her outfit and headed straight for the boardroom. When she pushed through the door, the talking stopped, and they all turned to look at her. She scrunched her nose.

"Sorry I'm late. I've had a day that no one could have prepared for."

"Looks that way," Brian Chandler, the CEO, said. He was looking at her hand, which held her shoes. Jenni rolled her eyes and took her seat.

"We don't need to discuss that." There was a scattering of snickering around the table of men and women around her. "Now, what did I miss?"

She released a breath, relieved she was finally sitting there and didn't have to think about everything that had gone wrong this morning. Though she tried to stop herself, her mind drifted back to the beautiful woman she had met a few moments earlier. Wedding ring or not, it didn't keep her from wanting to know more about her. Why had she been so sad? If Jenni saw her again, she wanted to at least get to know her. They could be friends, couldn't they?

CHAPTER THREE

Tabby

The sound of the beeping from the monitor ticked in time to the seconds on the clock over Holly Hutchinson's bed as Tabby documented the numbers from her machine. When she left the hospital the night before, she hadn't known Holly's name, but during the night, the woman had woken up. She had easily remembered facts, such as name and age and how to reach her family. The accident, on the other hand, was a whole other story; she couldn't remember a thing about it. But as doctors liked to point out, that wasn't necessarily a bad thing when the patient's mental status was normal. Sometimes blocking out trauma could work in a patient's favor.

Holly shifted in the bed and made a noise. Tabby looked at her, asking, "Do you need anything? Water?"

Holly shook her head, then dropped her eyes to look down

at her legs. Tabby slid her pen into the clipboard holder. It was her job to get Holly's mind on something else, anything else, other than what her body was going through. "My name is Tabby. I'll be the head nurse assigned to your case. It looks like you had a long night, but I'm glad to see you're up and moving."

Holly scoffed. "Moving, right. As I see it, I may never walk again."

"You don't know that. You'll be put through extensive therapy, and we're going to do everything we can to get movement back into your legs. Just think positively because none of us will think otherwise until we've exhausted all measures." Holly nodded, then winced and shifted in her bed. "Are you in pain?" Tabby asked.

"A little," she mumbled. Tabby pressed the button on her IV pump to administer a dose of pain medication.

"In a few minutes, you'll start to feel much better. If you need anything, be sure to press the button for a nurse. Just try to relax. We're going to do everything we can for you. Got that?"

Holly nodded, then closed her eyes. She needed rest. Tabby finished her paperwork and quietly left her room. As she headed to the front desk, she spotted Hanna sitting at the computer and waved, but her friend's eyes were looking elsewhere. Tabby turned and noticed that the woman from earlier was slowly walking to the front door, mostly distracted by her phone. Her shoes were no longer in her hands, so that was a good thing. Perhaps she had thrown them away. Tabby, though, would have probably found a way to get that broken heel fixed. Money didn't come easily, and the shoes were leopard print and looked to be real leather.

Tabby approached the desk, and Hanna turned her attention to her. "How's Holly doing?"

"I'd say a tad depressed. Think we'd better monitor that."

Hanna nodded. "When I was in her room this morning before you got here, I talked briefly to her. I got the same vibe, so good call." Hanna went on to punch something on the computer.

Tabby looked toward the door where Jenni stood, still on her phone.

"Who is that woman, by the way?" Tabby asked, pointing toward the door.

Hanna looked up. "Do you mean Jennifer Jennison?" She smirked. "Even her name gives you the vibes of 'rich and powerful,' right?"

Tabby chuckled. "I've never met the woman until today. I bumped into her when I was coming in. She wasn't paying attention. Or I wasn't. Either way, head-on collision."

"I'm not really surprised. Jenni is always in a rush."

"You seem to know her well, like you're on a first-name basis."

Hanna stood, shrugging. "Guess you could say we've been friendly through the years. It's not like we do anything outside of the hospital, but I met her once, and now we're BFFs inside the hospital." She laughed. "I'm partly teasing. Anyway, mind if I go to lunch?"

Tabby shook her head and watched as Hanna left the ER. Jennifer Jennison was one of those women everyone knew was rich and powerful. It was no secret that she had put a lot of money into Capmed. Yet, it was more of a behind-the-scenes endeavor, which was why Tabby hadn't recognized her. It was rumored that others had seen Jenni in passing, but in all the five years that Jenni had invested money in the hospital, Tabby had never crossed paths with her. She wondered why she was seeing this woman twice in one day.

Tabby looked over at Jenni again, who was still completely engrossed with her phone. She rolled her neck with a sigh and a strand of hair slipped from her bun. There wasn't anything unusual about it, but a sudden urge flared in Tabby to cross the distance between them and tuck the hair back in place. She'd never paid attention to how attractive another woman was, but something about Jenni drew her in. She carried herself with ease, even when rushing, and she had kind, friendly eyes. But when they had bumped into each other earlier, she had sensed a bit of sadness behind Jenni's gaze— the same sadness inside Tabby.

As Tabby continued staring, she noticed how Jenni's hips curved beautifully in the skirt she wore. Jenni was pretty, but Tabby wasn't sure why she was noticing that so much. The desk phone at the nurses' station rang, startling her. She picked it up, watching Jenni saunter away. "This is Tabby Brickly. May I help you?"

"Mom?"

Callie's voice came on to the phone, and Tabby smiled and leaned back in her seat. "Hey, Callie, what's going on? Are you at school?"

"Yeah, but Jamie let me borrow her cell. You know she's my age, right? She's had a cell phone for two years. Don't you think—"

"Callie," Tabby stated sternly.

"Yes, Mom?"

"We've been through this before. Brittany only just got a phone, and if we were to get you one, that wouldn't look right. You know that."

"Times are a-changing, Mom," Callie argued.

Tabby covered her mouth, stifling a laugh at that archaic response coming from her nine-year-old daughter. Someone had clearly put that phrase into her head. As far as Tabby was concerned, she wasn't ready for her little girl to be growing up so fast. The longer she could keep Callie from wanting to have all the things her older sister had, the better.

"I'm sure you didn't borrow the phone just to rehash over how you're not getting a phone, at least for a few years. Or did you?"

"Right. Anyway, I was just checking to see if you were going to be home for supper tonight. You left early, so I'm hoping you are. I thought I would cook for everyone. It's chicken mar...mar...mar...ugh. I don't remember what Mrs. Davies called it, but it was sooo good yesterday when we made it in class."

Tabby snickered. "What happened to the highlight of your day being recess? You're now making meals? And was it chicken marsala?"

"That's it," she squealed.

Tabby smiled and shook her head. "Honey, that sounds amazing, but we'd have to stop by the grocery store. I doubt we have the ingredients."

"But, Mom," Callie whined.

"I'll tell you what," Tabby began. "I'll be home at six

tonight. Let me make supper. Then this weekend you and I will go to the store, and you can buy all the ingredients you want. How does that sound?"

"Okay, I guess," Callie muttered. "I love you!"

"Love you, too. Have a great rest of your day at school. I'll see you when I get home." Tabby dropped the phone into the receiver and stared at it. Moments like that were when she knew that she would do anything to provide for her daughters.

When Tabby had first started working at Capmed, she was eighteen, a brand-new mom, and in need of a job that would help with tuition reimbursement. She had worked as a lab tech, monitoring the front desk and organizing files for the department. She had wanted a career that would give her family financial independence, and it had worked out. Plus, she was able to help save lives. It put her life in perspective when she came home at night and only had cereal for supper. If she weren't doing it all to help others and benefit her daughters' lives, it would be an easier choice to walk away from her career. She wanted to be home every night, mothering her kids, helping them with homework, and cooking supper for her family. It just wasn't realistic. So Capmed was where she was going to be, as long as it would help her provide for those she loved.

❦

Tabby walked into Joanna Kinner's room. Her patient sat on the edge of the bed, her daughter right beside her, gripping her hand. "Well, are you all set to leave? How do you feel, Joanna?"

"Pretty good," she said. "Maybe a little nervous, but I'm anxious to be going home. It's been a few weeks since I've been able to walk into my own house. I feel ready, but does the doctor think I'm ready to go?"

Tabby smiled at her. "If the doctors were at all hesitant, you would be spending a few more days in that bed. Just enjoy it." She held out a packet of paperwork, and her daughter took it. "In there is a prescription for some medicine. If you have any chest pain, return to the hospital immediately. If you experience nausea, do the same. We're not leaving you out there unattended. You should follow up with your primary care physician in three to five days so they have your records. Do you have any questions for me?"

Joanna shook her head, still looking hesitant. She was eighty-nine years old, and from talking to her daughter, Sidney, Tabby knew she was worried that she would never get to go home to her three beloved cats. Tabby was relieved to see that they could keep their promise to get Joanna out of the hospital.

"How about you, Sidney? Any questions?"

Sidney looked up and met Tabby's gaze, then shook her head. "Thank you," she said, standing up and hugging Tabby, "for everything. We're glad you were here."

Tabby smiled warmly. "You're welcome. Your discharge is complete. Patient transport will wheel you out to the front. Let me lead the way." She walked ahead, leading them out of the hospital room and to the nurses' station, where Becca, another nurse, sat at the computer. "Becca, if you could, please sign Joanna out. They're good to go."

She reached out and squeezed Joanna's hand. "Don't hesitate to reach out to us for any reason. You're not in this alone. I'll see you guys around."

"Hopefully not too soon," Joanna replied, smiling.

Tabby nodded and turned away, heading back into the room to clean up in case a new patient needed a bed. When she finished, she left and headed toward the next patient she needed to check up on. She turned a corner and stopped. Jenni, in sleek black high heels, a tight-fitting skirt, blouse, and black jacket, was walking straight toward her. She hadn't noticed Tabby, since she was focused on her phone yet again.

Tabby swallowed as Jenni got close enough that she could smell her perfume. Jenni quickly sidestepped so they didn't have another collision, and Tabby cleared her throat. "Uh, you look like you're lost."

The woman looked up, eyes widening in recognition. A smile grew on her face. "Not lost. At least I have both my heels on today." She looked down at her feet.

Tabby nodded. "I noticed."

Jenni quirked an eyebrow. "Oh? You were looking at my feet?"

Tabby's cheeks burned. Why was she suddenly hit with embarrassment? She tried to look away, wondering if she should get back to work, but Jenni had a grin that just wouldn't quit, and Tabby found herself studying the woman's lips.

"It's not that I was looking," Tabby quickly responded. "I mean, I just happened to be looking down when you headed this way. That's all." It was a good save—hopefully, a believable one. Jenni nodded, and Tabby released a breath.

"We haven't been introduced. I'm Jenni Jennison."

Jenni gave her name with such confidence it made Tabby

shrink inside. She was embarrassed to mutter her own last name. Yet, it was better than her maiden name, Char. "Tabitha, uh, Brickly," she said. "Or, I answer to Tabby, if you'd prefer."

The woman grinned. "Tabby it is." She held out her hand, and Tabby shook it. Jenni's grip was firm, warm, and inviting. Part of Tabby expected Jenni to go into details about finances and how she gave donations aplenty to Capmed, but instead, Jenni said, "I had a cat named Tabby when I was four years old."

Tabby was so embarrassed, she wanted to crawl under the desk. She wasn't sure how she was going to respond to something like that. Luckily, she didn't have to, since Jenni started laughing.

"I was wondering how you'd respond to that. Looking back, I realize that it wasn't quite the icebreaker I expected." She laughed loudly, and suddenly Tabby didn't mind. Jenni had an infectious laugh, and if that's what ended the awkwardness, then she would graciously accept it.

"Actually, I had a cat named Jenni," Tabby replied. Jenni stopped laughing, and her jaw dropped. Tabby shook her head. "Gotcha."

Jenni chortled, and for a few minutes in that hallway, everything that Tabby needed to accomplish before her day was over vanished. Jenni was captivating and gave her a sense of comfort she'd been lacking in her life for a long time. She was happy to linger in the hallway with Jenni just a few more minutes before the stress of work and life came flooding back in.

CHAPTER FOUR

Jenni

The sound of Tabby's laugh was like the sun coming out on a rainy day. When Jenni heard it, it made her want to smile. It brought her joy, and after the past couple of days she had had, she certainly could use that right about now.

"I have to get back to work," Tabby said. She waved, and Jenni nodded and moved past her.

Jenni turned to get one last glimpse, lingering around a corner, where she could quickly hide if Tabby noticed. Jenni watched as Tabby spoke to a patient waiting outside a room. Even from a distance, Jenni could see the kindness in Tabby's eyes and the respectful way she treated her patients. Of course a warmth like that would draw Jenni in.

A knot formed in the pit of her stomach. *What about Wendy?*

With a sigh, she left the area and continued down the hallway, heading straight for Dr. Charles Richards's office. She tapped on his door, then turned to look back to where she had left Tabby. She was busying herself at a computer, oblivious to Jenni watching her. She tapped again on the door.

"He's not in there."

Jenni looked to her right and smirked. "Apparently not, because he's right there in front of me." Jenni stepped away from the door. "Thought I would see if you were working today."

"Aren't I always?" he asked, opening his door. She followed him into his office. "Have a seat. I have a few minutes."

Jenni sunk into the chair facing his desk. Since she had started shelling donations into the hospital, she had become friends with Charles and his wife, Cecilia. He had become a confidant she could talk to when she was dealing with hospital matters, and it was nice to have someone there that she could work alongside when it seemed like everyone else looked down on her. A few people frowned upon the fact that she was part of the board of directors. She had become friendly with a couple of members of the board, but there was always that nagging thought that people didn't think she belonged there. Sometimes, she thought that was true. Her wife had always been the charismatic one with a strong influence. Jenni was there only by default.

"What's going on?" he asked. "You look like you have a heaviness weighing on your heart."

She smiled. "That sounds like something your wife puts in those romance novels she writes."

He laughed. "Maybe that's where I got it from." He leaned back in his chair and clasped his hands behind his head. "Still, it works in this situation. What's running around that mind of yours?"

Jenni sighed, desperate to let out all her thoughts. She wanted to be honest, but sometimes she worried that being completely honest wouldn't be appropriate. She was needed for her donations, but was never asked for her input on hospital matters. Her biggest fear was that she knew nothing about the medical community, so why try to pretend she did?

"Have you heard anything about what's going on with the hospital?" she asked.

Charles shrugged. "I know they're talking about expansions. It's a good thing, though. This place hasn't been renovated in over thirty years. I know that I, for one, will be happy to see this place improved."

"Well, it's more than that," Jenni said.

A knock on the door interrupted them. "Come in!" Charles hollered.

Jenni turned to see Tabby at the door. Tabby's eyes widened in surprise and confusion at seeing Jenni sitting across from Dr. Richards. "Hey, Tabby," Jenni greeted

"Hello," Tabby said, straightening her gaze from Jenni's. "Sorry to interrupt, Dr. Richards," she said.

"No worries, Tabitha."

"Ms. Rivers is complaining about chills and chest pain. She doesn't have a fever, but she asked if we could increase her meds. What do you think?"

He took the chart from Tabby and examined it. While they mused over it, Jenni looked over at Tabby. Her eyes never once swayed from looking at the chart, so Jenni's gaze went unnoticed.

"Yes, let's go ahead and add a transdermal nitroglycerin patch every six hours. Thanks, Tabitha."

"You're welcome, Doctor." Tabby nodded at Jenni. "Sorry again for the interruption." She quickly left the office, and Jenni looked toward the door as it closed.

"What do you know about her?" Jenni asked, turning back to Charles.

He tilted his head. "Well, not a whole lot. I try not to get too involved with the nurses who work in my ward. But I can say that I know she's married."

Jenni rolled her eyes. "The wedding ring told me that. Happily? To a man?"

Charles laughed and leaned back in his overstuffed chair. "What happened to *I'll never fall in love again?*"

"Who said anything about love?" Jenni crossed her legs. "I'm merely curious. I did just meet the woman, after all."

Charles nodded. "Married to a man. She has either one or two kids. That's the extent of my knowledge. She's a great nurse, but I doubt that was what you were thinking about when you were staring."

Jenni frowned, slightly abashed. Though she had to admit she found Tabby stunning, there was something beneath the surface she was drawn to. "Tabby seems like a warm, genuine person, and she's easy to talk to. I can tell she's a great nurse."

Jenni smiled. "But that brings us back to what I was saying earlier, as to what's happening here."

"Ahh, yes. Other than the expansions, of course. Do tell."

Jenni heaved a sigh, dreading what she was about to say. "They're cutting staffing funds. People are going to lose their jobs. They're doing a pretty hefty hack, too."

Charles's eyes narrowed. "Not my job, I hope."

"They aren't talking about doctor staffing—as of yet. They're saying they'll start with people who have been here the longest and work down the line."

He frowned. "How does that even make sense? We're going to lose our most seasoned employees?"

"They get paid the higher bucks, and they're trying to shave those off." She shrugged. "I don't agree with it, and a lot of people are going to lose their jobs over it. The economy is struggling right now. This is only going to make things tougher on everyone."

He shook his head. "And there's nothing that can be done?"

Jenni had considered that numerous times since getting the news the day before, but it seemed like an impossible feat to save all of the employees. She shrugged despondently. "I don't think there is."

"That's a bummer," Charles said. "It's going to put a burden on everyone, though, including the staff—heck, especially the doctors."

Jenni nodded. That was another thing to think about, but the board seemed adamant that was the only course of action. She hoped that it never came down to that, but if it did, then she would have to accept it.

"Enough negativity. How are Cecilia and your little rugrats?"

He smiled. "Ornerier than ever, and the kids are, too." He laughed and reached for a picture that was framed on his desk and holding it up. "The kids aren't so little, though. Not anymore." His eyes shone brightly, and Jenni smiled. "But they ask about Auntie Jenni often, so you might want to pay them a visit."

"I'll definitely have to make sure to do that," she said, still grinning.

There was once a time when Jenni thought she would be one of those doting parents who flashed pictures around when others inquired about her kids. That obviously hadn't worked out, but she didn't want people to see how much that bothered her. It was just the hand she had been dealt. There wasn't any reason to feel sad about it. Her years with Wendy, even though they hadn't had kids, were something she would never change. It was best to pretend nothing bothered her. She had grown used to doing that.

The microwave dinged, and Jenni opened the door and pulled her TV dinner out. She dropped it on the counter and grabbed her silverware, then carried everything to the kitchen table.

It was what her life had been reduced to over the years. When she first got out of college, she thought living a single life would be pure bliss, allowing her to do what she wanted and be who she wanted, and never have to apologize for it. That all changed when she met Wendy. It was an accident that had brought them together, a fender bender in a suburban neighborhood. Wendy was only two blocks from her home when she had swerved to keep from hitting a dog, and wound up hitting Jenni's car. At first, Jenni wasn't pleased. She was determined to read the riot act to the person who hadn't been paying attention and rammed into her. She hadn't seen the dog, but when she saw Wendy, nothing else mattered.

Wendy had sparked something deep and passionate inside her. Wendy was caring and a joy to be around, and her smile was infectious. She had a way of putting Jenni at ease, even after a stressful day. Three years later, they were married.

Jenni took her last bite of her TV dinner. It wouldn't last all night, but she would grab something to snack on before she headed off to bed. This was her life and routine. Why change that now?

She got up, tossed the container into the trash, and went to the living room, where a photo album sat on a coffee table. Jenni sat down on the couch and grabbed the album. She flipped it open to her wedding pictures.

It was the happiest day of their lives. Wendy was the most beautiful bride that had ever walked down the aisle. With her dark auburn hair and green eyes, she captivated everyone, but especially Jenni. She couldn't imagine her life without Wendy and the warmth she brought to everyone who knew her. Their dreams stemmed from getting married and starting a family. It was a struggle, though, spending so much time finding ways to get the baby they wanted. They had been hopeful when they tried in vitro fertilization, using the sperm from one of Wendy's coworkers. That had turned into another bust, leaving them more devastated than ever.

They had started the adoption process when the unthinkable happened. Wendy was T-boned coming home from work one night at her waitressing gig and died on impact. It was a drunk driver—a kid only eighteen years old. In the blink of an eye, two lives ended that night. The problem was that Jenni didn't know if she could ever start living, or loving, again. It felt like a betrayal of her true love.

She closed the album and put it back down on the coffee table. She could always hear Wendy's words in her head. If anything ever happens to me, I need you to promise me something. Promise me you'll move on. I don't want to be in Heaven knowing that you're not living, and I will haunt you. So, promise me.

Back then, Jenni always thought that when she had made that promise, she would never actually need to keep it. Wendy would never know.

Jenni was forty when Wendy took her last breath. It had taken a long time, but things had slowly started to improve. Now, at forty-five, she wanted to try to keep that promise to her. So, when she first saw Tabby, she was taken aback. A spark she thought died with Wendy had suddenly been reignited. Tabby was the first woman Jenni had met, other than Wendy, whom she felt this instant connection with.

Jenni brushed the tears from her eyes and leaned back in her seat. Was it time for her to finally move on and let Wendy go? The only thing was, she wanted it to be with someone who would reciprocate those feelings with her. Her feelings for Tabby were doomed, since Tabby was married. Jenni looked down at the cover of the photo album. A beaming picture of both Wendy and Jenni on the cover stared back at her. "I know you want me to be happy, Wendy. I'm trying, baby."

She stood up from the couch and headed to her bedroom. It wasn't easy spending nights alone, but maybe one day she'd fulfill her promise to Wendy and find a new love. If only she could allow herself to move on.

CHAPTER FIVE

Tabby

C allie shifted in bed as Tabby leaned over her, tucking her in nice and tight. "How's that?" Tabby asked.

"Perfect." Callie shifted her gaze to her light, then back to Tabby. "Mom?"

"Yes, Peaches?" Tabby asked.

Callie's grin widened. "You haven't called me that since I was in kindergarten."

Tabby laughed. "If memory serves me, that's when you said you were too old to have a nickname. Since we're alone, I didn't think you'd mind."

Callie quickly shook her head. "Mom? Tonight was good. You know, you being home and making supper. Like we were a real family."

Tabby sat down on the edge of her daughter's bed. "Well, we are a real family."

Callie giggled. "I know, but it has been a while. I liked it. I'm sure Brittany did, too."

"Well, I'll tell you something." Tabby leaned in, her breath warm as she caressed her daughter's cheek and rested her lips on her ear. "I did, too."

Callie giggled and held out her arms so they could embrace. It was moments like these, tucking her daughter into bed and having these sweet conversations with her, that Tabby treasured.

"Now, you get some sleep, little one." Tabby stood up from her bed. "We'll go shopping this weekend, and you can make your dish for the whole family."

Callie clapped her hands and beamed. "Love you!"

"Love you too, Peaches. Sweet dreams." She looked over at her as Callie shifted in bed and turned, her back facing the door. Tabby turned off her light and left her room. As she stepped into the hallway, she heard the faint sound of Drew's guitar coming from downstairs. She heaved a sigh and moved to Brittany's room. She tapped on the door before opening it. Brittany was in her bed, pulling her earbuds from her ears as Tabby entered.

"Hey, Mom."

"Hey, sweetheart. Are you going to get ready for bed?"

Brittany groaned. "I'm thirteen and surely don't need the same bedtime as my younger sister."

Tabby chuckled. "Well, it is Friday night, so I suppose you have a point there. What are you listening to?"

Brittany arched an eyebrow. "Grunge. You wouldn't understand it."

Tabby let out another laugh. "You're probably right." Kids nowadays were a lot different from when Tabby was a kid. It didn't even seem like that long ago. Some days she felt like she had to grow up so fast at seventeen that she had lost her youth in the process. It was hard to fathom that she had been only four years older than Brittany was when she bore her first child.

"Did you like what we had for dinner?" Tabby asked.

Brittany's eyes shone as she nodded. "It was good. Even better that you were there to enjoy it with us."

That was the consensus for all three of them. "I'm glad I was here, too." Tabby walked over to Brittany and kissed her forehead. "I know you're nearly an adult," she teased, "but don't stay up too late."

Brittany smiled as Tabby walked away. "Night, Mom."

"Goodnight." Tabby blew her a kiss and left the room. The music still played downstairs, and Tabby hesitated at her own bedroom. She wanted to just slip into her room, fall asleep, and not have to face her husband. With a sigh, she headed for his music room.

Drew had been quiet at dinner. While she and the kids had chatted about school, he had seemed to be in his own little world. Tabby wondered what was on his mind that had kept him so quiet. As she drew closer to the music room, the guitar playing got louder, then stopped when she stepped into Drew's sanctuary. He had his head down as he wrote something down. Tabby was hesitant to interrupt him, and after watching him for some time, he started to play again.

She remembered vividly the first time she saw him playing.

She was sixteen years old, and she had thought it was the coolest thing. She had never thought she would one day wind up meeting him, hooking up with him on that winter night, and ultimately finding herself in a position to get married. She had thought it was love at first sight. And in many ways, she had walked down the aisle, to the altar, feeling that way, too. But looking back, it was more the thrill of Drew being a bad boy. Her parents had disapproved of him from the get-go, but Tabby had wanted to prove them wrong and prove to herself that she could have an amazing family of her own.

Drew stopped strumming and went back to writing something on his music sheet. "If you're going just to stare…" he started.

"I didn't want to interrupt," she said.

He looked up. "Too late for that."

His snarky response would have normally sent her running out of the room, but if she couldn't have a civil conversation with him, then maybe they were going about this all the wrong way.

"You were quiet at dinner," she said.

He sighed and looked away, shaking his head. "What do you want me to say, Tab?" he asked, turning back to face her. "Do you want me to praise you for making it to one dinner? Is that it? Do you realize these kids are your responsibility, too? And yet, you stay out all hours of the night and expect me to be Mr. Mom. Well, you made it home for one dinner. Bravo." He clapped, and Tabby stared at him, frustration coursing through her veins. She willed the tears not to fall. It wouldn't help anything if she started crying. It would only egg him on and add to her torment.

"It's not like I'm out carousing the neighborhood like a stray cat. I'm working. I'm trying to give this family the life they expect. I'm bringing home the money, Drew. I don't see your hobby paying the bills."

His eyes darted up to hers, and his jaw hung slightly. "Nice." He shook his head. "I can't believe you just said that to me. You used to love that I played music. But now you think my job is just a hobby?"

"Drew," Tabby started. "I didn't mean it the way it came out. I understand your passion, and I want you to follow that passion and go wherever it leads you. Unfortunately, it hasn't led you to paying gigs. That's a problem, so it makes me strive to get in more hours of work. Otherwise, we're looking at losing electricity and water. Is that what you want for your kids?"

A groan came from him, and he shot her another look. "You know it isn't. I love those kids, and I love you. You know that."

Tabby nodded, swallowing the lump in her throat. It'd been a while since he said those words to her. Yet she hadn't been able to say them to him, either. So, it wasn't like it was one-sided. She wanted to believe it was love that kept her from leaving, but lately, she wasn't so sure.

"It's getting late. The kids are in bed, and maybe we should just go to bed, too."

He shook his head and looked down at his music. "I have work to do. It might just be a hobby to you, but I'm working to make it more. If you were home more often, you would know this. I'll head up later," he grumbled.

"All right," Tabby said despondently.

She left his music room and went up the stairs, her heart breaking with each step she took. Giving him space seemed to be something she had to do every night. The more space she gave him, the bigger the wedge between them. It was too much to believe they could fix it.

As she lay in bed, attempting to get some sleep, the sound of Drew's guitar continued to filter through the vents. If she could hear it, she was confident her kids could, too. The only saving grace was that they were heavy sleepers and hopefully already dead to the world.

***

Time seemed to tick slowly by, but what could Tabby do to change his mind if Drew didn't want to come upstairs? She tossed and turned, hoping to fall asleep, because she needed some rest, and Drew did, too. Yet he remained downstairs, just strumming on his guitar. At one point, he even started playing his harmonica. That's when Tabby grabbed his pillow and pushed it down on her face, hoping it would muffle the music. No such luck. She placed the pillow down and sat up.

"Two thirty?" she mumbled, floored that Drew was trying to prove a point that kept him going into the morning. What respect did that provide her children? None, in Tabby's opinion.

If Drew was trying to prove a point, he had done it. He wanted to turn his hobby into a full-time gig. She got that, but this wasn't changing anything. She tossed the covers back and slipped out of bed, trying to salvage at least some sleep by telling Drew to stop.

The music stopped. Tabby hesitated at the door, then heard footsteps coming up the stairs. She hurried back to the bed and got back under the covers. A moment later, the door opened.

"You're still awake," Drew mumbled.

Tabby sat up in bed. "I didn't think you were ever going to come to bed."

He went over to a chair and grabbed his lounge pants and T-shirt. He looked over at her and shrugged. "Needed a break."

"From me?" Tabby asked.

He heaved a sigh. "Tab, I'm tired of arguing all the time. So, yeah, from you. From us. From marriage. From life."

"Wow," Tabby muttered, tossing the covers back aggressively.

"Where are you going?" he asked as she reached the door.

Tabby slowly turned to face him. "You're not the only one who needs a break. I'm trying to hold on to this marriage, and you're trying to push me away, saying you need a break? How do you think that makes me feel? I'll tell you how, like my feelings are worth nothing."

He snorted, making Tabby step backward. If he didn't want to appreciate that she was trying, then maybe she could do nothing to fix this.

"I don't see you trying." He looked up and met her gaze. "If you were, then you would make sure to be home every night to fix us supper. You would change your hours to accommodate your family. But you're not."

"It's not that simple, Drew." She looked away from him, then moved farther out the door. "But you'll never get it, right? I need some air." She turned and hurried down the stairs. The moment she stepped outside, she slammed the door behind her. Tears were brimming on the edge of her eyes, and she flicked them off. *Don't cry, Tabby. It's what he wants.*

What was it that she wanted, though? If only she could figure that out herself, then maybe she wouldn't be stuck in a marriage that was failing right in front of her. She turned and looked up at the window that peered into their bedroom, seeing Drew's shadow. The moment she locked eyes with him, he shut the window curtain. That was the story of their love. It was slowly fading away.

Tabby entered the market with her daughters and looked over at Callie. "The grocery store is all yours. I'll grab the cart, and you put in what you need."

"I can't believe you're letting a nine-year-old feed us," Brittany muttered. "What if we get sick? What if we die?"

Tabby ruffled her daughter's hair. "Don't be so dramatic." She leaned against her ear. "I'll be there along the way—no worries."

The look on Brittany's face still indicated she was worrying, but she nodded as Tabby grabbed the cart, and they followed Callie through the store. One by one, Callie tossed items into the cart, and Tabby's mind went back to the previous night. The arguments with Drew weren't the worst they had ever had, but still, it was tough to just be okay with it. After twelve years of marriage, she wanted to do what she could to get through the rough patches, but it was getting harder to maneuver through them.

Callie reached an aisle and peered through the rows of bottles. Tabby jerked herself out of her reverie and looked at her. "What are you doing?"

"The recipe says Marsala wine. I've never shopped for wine before. Do you know where it is?" She looked up, hopeful.

Tabby grabbed the recipe from her and looked down at it, then at Callie in amusement. "It can be left out. Let me rephrase that. In this case, it will be left out."

"Mom," she groaned. "I want everything to be perfect."

"And it will be." Tabby raised an eyebrow. "But we're not putting wine in this recipe. Got it?" Her tone was stern, and she bit down on her lip—no need in taking out her frustration with her kids. "I promise you," she said, brushing her hand under Callie's chin, "it will still taste amazing."

Callie groaned again, but nodded. Tabby handed the list back to her and sighed, shaking her head. At least she was coherent enough to have prevented that from going into the cart. She turned and pushed the cart into another cart next to a woman looking at the shelves.

"Sorry about that," Tabby said.

The woman turned, and Tabby's eyes widened when she realized who it was. "Hello there," Jenni said.

"Hi. Didn't see you there." Tabby turned to her two children, who had suddenly grown shy. She wrapped an arm around her two daughters. "This is my daughter Brittany," Tabby said, motioning her hand over Brittany's head. "And this is my daughter Callie."

Jenni nodded. "Pleasure to meet you both."

"And this is Jenni. She has business dealings with Capmed." She cringed. Was that even an accurate way to describe Jenni's relationship with the hospital? She looked at her two children, who simply nodded and cowered behind her. She smiled. "They're more of the introverted type."

Jenni smiled wider. "I know the feeling. I am, too."

She spoke directly to both Tabby's children, and Tabby relaxed when she saw both girls smile. "Callie is making dinner tonight for all of us. It'll be her first time preparing the whole meal."

"Oh? Nice," Jenni replied. "How old are you, Callie?"

Tabby opened her mouth to respond for Callie, but Callie seemed more at ease. "Nine. I'll be ten in thirty-four days."

Tabby chuckled. "Not that she's counting or anything."

Jenni grinned. "That's a big endeavor for someone so young." That made Callie smile even wider. "And how old are you?" she asked, looking over at Brittany.

"Thirteen," Brittany quickly answered.

"Ahh, to be a teenager again."

Brittany nodded, perking up.

"How old are you?" Callie blurted out.

Tabby wanted to duck into a corner as she placed her hand over Callie's mouth. "Kids say the darndest things," she said sheepishly.

Jenni laughed loudly, then knelt closer to Callie. "Forty-five. I know, super old. Don't tell anyone."

Tabby appreciated that Jenni spoke to her kids as if they were on the same level rather than treating them as immature children. It was nice to see another adult acting that way. And it impressed her that Jenni hadn't flinched when Callie had asked how old she was.

She remembered days when she, the kids, and Drew ran errands together. Their daughters were a lot younger, but they had actually spent and enjoyed time as a family, laughing and exploring the world. Now, she didn't know who Drew was anymore.

Jenni was so different. While Drew always seemed to be looking through her, Jenni gave Tabby her full attention, smiling and speaking kindly. What a contrast to Drew's snarky responses and awful attitude.

She imagined how being with Jenni would make her so much happier.

She bit her lip and looked at her feet. Jenni was making her think all kinds of strange thoughts. She'd never considered being with another woman, but there was something about Jenni...

"Um, we should get going," Tabby said, trying to maintain her composure, though her heart was beating a mile a minute because of Jenni's proximity. "It was good to see you."

"You too, Tabby. Nice to meet you, Brittany and Callie." As Jenni passed, she touched Tabby's shoulder and gave it a soft squeeze, which sent a jolt through Tabby.

As Jenni went to another aisle, Brittany and Callie grinned, no longer the shy individuals they were five minutes ago.

Tabby tried to calm her racing heart as Callie continued to grab things for her dish, and they paid and left the store. As the three loaded the groceries into the trunk of their car, Tabby's phone dinged from a text message.

"Finish up, girls," she said, grabbing her phone and looking down at Drew's message.

I need some space tonight. I won't be home until late. Don't wait up.

Tabby typed back furiously, *What? Your daughter is making supper. You're going to miss that?*

Don't get all high and mighty with me. It's not like you haven't missed plenty of meals.

None that our daughter was making.

Differences…differences…make an excuse for me.

Incredulous, Tabby pocketed her phone. She couldn't believe she was about to make an excuse for Drew for whatever he felt was more important than Callie's dinner. She pocketed her phone. If he didn't want to be there, he didn't want to be there.

"Is something wrong, Mom?" Brittany asked when they had all loaded into the vehicle.

Tabby forced a smile and looked in the rearview mirror. She couldn't stand seeing the smile fade from either of her daughter's faces, but especially Callie's. She watched Callie in the backseat, wondering what Drew had deemed to be more important than sharing in his daughter's meal.

"Unfortunately, your father has somewhere he needs to be tonight."

Callie turned and caught her gaze in the mirror. "He's not going to be there for my meal?"

Tabby shook her head. Damn you, Drew. "He has a sick friend he's looking after tonight. He says he's really sorry he won't be able to be there, but we'll keep some leftovers for him."

That brought a smile to Callie's face, and Tabby turned

back to the front to pull out of the parking spot. She looked over and saw Brittany staring at her intently. Tabby forced a smile of her own, hoping her daughter bought it, then continued her route to the house. Even if it was to protect Drew, lying was better than seeing the disappointment on Callie's face.

When they got to the house, the three of them worked to unload the groceries. When Callie stepped away to grab more bags, Brittany reached out for Tabby's arm, halting her. "Are you lying?" she asked. "About Dad helping out a friend, I mean?"

"We don't need to get into this now," Tabby replied, turning to look at her elder daughter.

"Mom, I'm not a kid. I know that you and Dad have been experiencing some difficult times." Tabby opened her mouth, but Brittany continued. "Do you know that most of my friends have divorced parents?"

Tabby's voice softened. "No, honey, I did not know that."

"They're thriving just fine." She shrugged. "Most of them, anyway." She turned to leave the kitchen to help Callie with the rest of the bags. Tabby stood there, shocked by Brittany's precociousness. If her kids were aware of their issues, then she and Drew weren't fooling anyone, but this was one more thing she would need to discuss with her husband. They shouldn't bring their children into their mess unless they were ready to make some big changes. Letting their daughters down was the last straw, in Tabby's mind. It was time to have a talk with Drew.

CHAPTER SIX

Jenni

J enni's head pounded as she rounded the corner. She fell back against a wall and started to massage her temples. *Just an hour,* she silently pleaded. *That's all you need to give me to get out of the hospital and home. Then I can rest all night. Please, pain, just an hour.*

She had been working for five hours, and she found herself plagued by a migraine that threatened to make her throw up. The lights in the hospital didn't help any, and the fact that she had left her medicine at home was just the cherry on top.

"Are you okay?"

She opened her eyes to see Tabby running up to her. Tabby reached for her arm, but Jenni straightened up and tried to force a smile. "Uh, yeah, I'm fine," she lied, gritting her teeth.

"You look like you're ready to pass out," Tabby said. "Come on."

Jenni leaned against her, and Tabby helped her into an empty room. "I'm fine," Jenni said again, even as Tabby helped her onto a bed.

"And I stand by the fact that you look anything but fine. Your color is completely faded from your cheeks."

Without warning, Tabby brushed her fingers against Jenni's cheeks in concern, and Jenni fought to not reach toward the soothing touch. If she wasn't already flushed, she'd be burning from the feel of Tabby's hand.

Tabby frowned and then felt Jenni's forehead. Jenni always felt a tad warm when she got migraines. They tended to affect her whole body.

"I just have a migraine. No biggie."

"Have you taken anything for it? If you have, it's not working." Tabby knelt in front of her, looking concerned. Tabby was a nurse; it was her job to be concerned. Yet Jenni couldn't shake the resulting warmth that bubbled inside her.

"I left my meds at home. I only have an hour left here, and then I'm headed out. It's not a problem."

"It doesn't look like it," Tabby said. "Wait here." She hurried out of the room and was only gone less than a minute before she returned with a cup of pills and bottled water. "Take this."

"Stealing drugs from the hospital? Someone could report you." Jenni joked weakly, quickly downing the pills. "I feel better already," she teased.

"At least you've got a sense of humor," Tabby replied. "This is a hospital. It makes no sense for people in pain not to get the relief they deserve. That's what meds are for. But don't worry, I didn't steal anything. These are from my private stash. It's the least I can do for my patient. And that's what you are right now—my patient."

"Oh, great," Jenni mock groaned. "I know what they charge here. My bill will be astronomical." She shook her head in jest and immediately regretted it as pain radiated through her whole body.

"We'll just say it's pro bono," Tabby replied. "Hopefully the meds will kick in soon, though. But seeing that this is a hospital, it makes me question why you didn't seek out help before you almost passed out in the hallway."

"I didn't want to bother anyone," Jenni quietly replied, glancing up at Tabby. She wasn't used to someone caring for her. For years, she'd been toughing everything out on her own. Now, Tabby was here showing her compassion and trying to help her feel better. Her heart fluttered.

"You donate money to this hospital, Jenni. You're not bothering anyone. Especially me." Tabby averted her gaze, looking a bit shy from such a bold statement.

She made a valid point, but Jenni had never thought of her assistance to Capmed as something that needed to be reciprocated. She didn't give the money because she wanted praise. She did it because she knew Wendy would want something good to come about from her death.

"So," Jenni started, trying to switch the topic from her migraine and on to anything else. "Did Callie end up making that dinner last Saturday? Your kids are adorable, by the way."

That brought a smile to Tabby's lips. "Thank you, and yes. I have to admit, she's not a bad chef. Might even be better than her mother." Tabby laughed. "She was happy to be cooking. I stayed in the kitchen, but…" She frowned suddenly. "Why are we talking about this?"

"Because when I don't think about my stupid migraine, I feel better," Jenni pointed out.

"Well, may I ask just one thing, and then we can drop it?" Tabby asked.

"If you must," Jenni sighed.

"How long have you gotten migraines, and have you ever had them observed?"

Jenni arched an eyebrow in mock disdain. "You just asked two things." She laughed and said, "I would say it's been going on twenty-five years, and I have had numerous doctors and specialists take a look, and they all say the same thing. I just need to deal with it." She shrugged. "So that's what I do. Deal with it. Now, back to Callie and her meal. What'd she cook?"

Tabby looked like she didn't want to drop the subject, but replied, "Chicken marsala. Without the Marsala." She grinned. "Callie was confused about why she couldn't have the wine in her dish. But it tasted good, nonetheless."

Jenni laughed, immediately forgetting her headache. "I was wondering why you were in the alcohol section. Both your daughters seem like sweet girls, by the way."

"They're the best," Tabby said. Her eyes darkened, and Jenni wanted to delve more into the topic of her family. She opened her mouth, but the door flew open, breaking into their conversation.

"Oh. Sorry," the nurse said, backing from the door.

"It's all right, Hanna." Tabby got up from the chair and looked over at Jennie. "Just finishing up here."

"Yeah, thanks so much, Tabby." Jenni jumped off the bed and scurried out of the room past Hanna and a patient. She didn't want Tabby to get into trouble. She somehow felt better, but that was more from just talking to Tabby rather than from the meds she had just taken. There was something soothing about being around Tabby, and she was left even more curious about her.

Jenni walked into the club and looked around. She was glad she no longer had a migraine and equated that to the fact that she had had a great conversation with Tabby and that she had gotten plenty of rest after. She spotted her best friend, Kim, engrossed in a conversation with a man who stood at a table. As she drew closer, she caught how strongly Kim was flirting with the guy. It was subtle to other people, but to someone who knew Kim so well, it was so obvious that it should have slapped the guy in the forehead.

He, however, seemed unaware. While he rattled off the specials, Kim batted her eyes in time with every drink from the list. Jenni rolled her eyes as she reached the table. Either he was clueless or just plain uninterested.

"The peach mango smoothie with a shot of tequila sounds heavenly," Kim cooed. "I'll take that. Unless you would suggest something else?"

"No, that's a fine choice, ma'am. Coming right up." He looked over at Jenni as she grabbed the seat across from Kim. "What can I get you, ma'am?"

"I'll take a beer, light. Thanks." He nodded and walked

away. Jenni turned to her friend, whom she hadn't seen in nearly a year. "You realize there are two problems with him, right?"

"He's a total babe and has a killer a...abs." She smirked. "What's the problem with that?"

Jenni shook her head. "He's no older than twenty-one, and he's probably gay."

"I'd be able to tell if he was gay," Kim protested. "My gaydar hasn't gone off once. As for the age, he's legal. It's clearly not something that would keep us from hooking up in the bathroom, or the alley, or on top of the stove in the kitchen. I'm not picky." She winked, and Jenni shook her head, unable to keep from smiling.

"I've missed you."

"I've missed you more, Jenni. Gosh. It's been way too long. How've you been? Tell me everything. I feel like way too much time has passed, and I'm dying to hear about everything."

Before Jenni could open her mouth, the waiter came back with their drinks. Kim looked in his direction. "My friend here and I have a bet going on, Coolio. Care to help us decipher the winner?"

"I'll do whatever I can, ma'am," he responded.

Kim tossed a look over to Jenni, and Jenni laughed silently. She didn't know what Kim was trying to prove, but whatever it was, it was sure to be entertaining.

"It's a two-parter," she continued. "How old are you, and are you gay or straight?"

Jenni covered her face and shook her head. Kim hadn't changed at all. They were best friends from first grade and had been inseparable until college. Then Kim decided to move to

California, which had worried Jenni. What if their friendship couldn't withstand the distance? She was glad to find that wasn't an issue as they continued to keep in contact with one another. Even though they didn't see each other often, they still talked frequently. But Kim was, by far, the bold one out of the two of them. Jenni would have never had the courage to ask the waiter such personal questions.

Coolio just smirked as he leaned onto the table. "Which one is betting I'm gay?" he asked, shifting his eyes from one to the other. Jenni pointed to Kim while Kim pointed in her direction. Jenni felt her face turning every shade of red, and she was ready to crawl under the table. Coolio just laughed.

"I'm twenty-two, and I am indeed gay. Does that settle it?" He winked and then left the table. Jenni watched Kim's eyes linger longer than necessary on Coolio's butt as he continued to walk away.

"Damn," she huffed, looking over to Jenni. "My gaydar was way off on that one."

Jenni took a sip of her beer. "Maybe next time you'll trust me. Besides, with a name like Coolio....Come on." She shook her head in jest and continued to drink her beer.

Kim laughed and shrugged. "Oh well. He's nice to look at, anyway."

Jenni smirked and looked around the room. Her eyes stopped just two tables from theirs. Sitting there were Tabby and some other women from the hospital. She quickly looked away.

"We should get something to eat. I'm famished." She kept her eyes focused on the menu, oblivious to the fact that Kim was scrutinizing her.

"Did you see something over there?" Kim asked. "You're all pale, like you saw a ghost or something." Jenni looked up as Kim looked over to Tabby's table.

"Stop it!" Jenni hissed, reaching out to grab her friend's hand. Kim looked back at her, eyebrows raised.

"Who's over there? Now your cheeks are all red." She leaned over the table, her eyes locked on Jenni's, firing off questions. "What's going on? Did you find someone? You look like you're ready to bolt. Is it someone at that table?"

She turned to look again, but Jenni grabbed Kim's hand. When Kim looked back, her jaw dropped. "It is. Who is it? The pretty redhead over there? The blonde with dazzling blue eyes?"

Jenni tilted her head. "We're not that close to them. How can you see their eye color?"

Kim shrugged. "Looks blue from over here. I could go and get a closer look." She started to get up, but Jenni kicked her under the table, and she laughed and fell back into her seat. "Come on, Jenni. You're withholding info from me. Who are you attracted to? I haven't seen this look on you in over five years."

Jenni rolled her eyes and looked down at her menu. "You're reading it all wrong," she lied.

"I think not," Kim replied. "A couple of them are headed this way. Is it either of them?"

Jenni looked up and stared straight at Tabby as she headed toward their table. Jenni pushed her hair behind her ear, hoping she didn't look awkward. "Hey, Hanna. Tabby." She put a smile on her lips but made sure to direct it toward Tabby especially.

"Thought that was you over here," Tabby said. She cast a look over at Kim, but Jenni didn't introduce her, and Kim didn't say anything. She quickly turned away. "Enjoy the rest of your night."

"Bye, Jenni," Hanna called out, then grabbed Tabby's hand and pulled her away from the table, heading in the direction of the dance floor.

Jenni caught herself looking at the floor as Hanna, Tabby, and a few of the other nurses danced. Kim cleared her throat, making Jenni look back in her direction.

"So was it the woman who was making googly eyes all over you?" Kim asked.

"What? She was not. For starters, she's married with two children."

Kim laughed. "You clearly knew which one I was referring to." She looked back down at the menu as Jenni sat there, nervously shifting in her seat. "Curly fries or crinkle?"

"I don't care," Jenni mumbled, closing her menu and pushing it away. She wasn't ready to eat and just wanted to pretend that interaction hadn't happened. She looked out on the dance floor again. No one was paying her any mind. Kim had definitely been mistaken when she said that Tabby was making eyes at her. Jenni shook her head. Why get caught up in some fantasy?

"Wanna talk about it?" Kim asked.

"Nothing to talk about," Jenni remarked. "Are you ready to order? You're only in town one night, and the last thing I want to discuss is how foolish I am."

"I hear you. We can always discuss that later," Kim replied jokingly.

"Yeah, yeah," Jenni said. She just wanted to forget that Kim had ever said anything and try to move past the evening. There wasn't anything between Jenni and Tabby, and the lack of eye contact from Tabby was proof. Logic and reason always differed from where Jenni's mind tended to stray, though, and as Tabby danced, Jenni's eyes remained glued to Tabby, imagining what it would be like to be dancing with her, and hoping that one day she would get the chance.

CHAPTER SEVEN

Tabby

A s much as Tabby was enjoying the night out with her work pals, she couldn't stop thinking about the girls. She and Drew really hadn't gotten anywhere, despite their attempt to talk after he had stayed out until three in the morning the previous Saturday. He had said he needed space, and Callie had seemed to forgive him, so Tabby decided it was best to ease up and accept it. But it was also the main reason she had decided to make her own escape from the house, if only temporarily. But now, she feared it was only hurting her daughters in the process.

"That was weird, didn't you think?" Hanna yelled over the music as they danced.

"Huh? What was weird?" She didn't want the women to think she was blowing them off by not being fully there with them. Since she had allowed them to whisk her off to the club, she would try to appreciate the time away. Yet, thoughts of Callie and Brittany wouldn't stop plaguing her mind.

"Jenni. I mean, we've talked in the past, but she's been around the hospital more often lately. And now, I'm seeing her at the club like it's a normal thing. It just seems strange, don't you think?"

Tabby looked over to the table, where Jenni was watching them dance. She quickly looked away. She wondered if Jenni was on a date, but tried to shrug that thought away. It wasn't her concern if she was. "Maybe she wants to have more of a role in the hospital. As for being here, I'm sure she goes out every once in a while. Everyone needs a life."

"I guess, but when she first got involved with the hospital, she was closed off. I heard something about her spouse dying. Strange that we've never really been filled in on her story."

"Well, maybe she's ready to make some changes." Again, Tabby shrugged. It all sounded plausible, and though she craved to learn as much about Jenni as she could, she worried about getting too close, especially with the strange feelings Jenni had been stirring lately. Jenni kept glancing over at her, so Tabby kept looking away, but she really liked how Jenni looked tonight. She wasn't used to seeing her in a dress. It really showed off her legs.

She frowned at herself. She had to stop thinking about Jenni so much. She was worried about her girls.

She glanced at her watch. It was only nine o'clock. It would be way too early to run home. She could already hear the ragging her friends would give her. She continued to dance, looking over at Ginger and Sally. They were dancing as if a slow song was playing. Then again, why not? They were happily in love, even sharing a kiss while they danced. Tabby smiled at them. She couldn't remember the last time she and Drew had shared a kiss in public. They barely kissed in private.

"I think I'm going to have to go," she said, turning to Hanna.

"You can't be serious. The night is still early."

"But my daughters…" she started.

Hanna reached out and touched her arm. "Is everything okay? You seem to be a bit rattled lately. If you have to go, then you have to go, but I don't want you leaving because you're not having fun. We could go somewhere else."

"It's not that…" Tabby started to argue. She paused when she felt her phone vibrating. She pulled it out of her pocket and looked at Hanna. "I'll be right back." Tabby hurried off the dance floor to a quiet place. "Hello?"

"Mom?" Callie's voice came onto the other end of the line.

She sighed. For a moment, she thought it would be Drew telling her there was a problem at the house. Hearing her daughter's voice was a relief. "Hey, it's past your bedtime. You know that, right?"

"When are you coming home?" she asked.

Hearing the heartbreak in her daughter's voice made Tabby think about running out right there.

"I said I would be home late, and your father would be tucking you in," Tabby responded. "Where's Brittany?"

"She's on the phone with a friend. Dad's busy with his stupid guitar."

"Put him on the phone, please." Tabby could feel the

blood curdling inside of her. She only wanted one night out with friends. She didn't think that was too much to ask when he had done the same. Or so she thought. She had never gotten a definitive response as to where he was that night. If he didn't respect her enough to offer up the truth, then why couldn't he at least give her some time to spend just doing her own thing? It was the least he could do.

"Yeah?" Drew's voice rang out.

"Drew? You promised me that I could hang with my friends tonight and that you would occupy the children so they didn't think about me not being there. What are you doing?"

"She wanted to talk to you. Is that a crime? We're fine. If you want to spend all night out, then go for it. I'll get her to bed. I'm not the one that called you. Remember that, dear, and don't pin this on me. Have a good time. I'm not saying you have to come home, by the way."

Tabby sighed. "Is Callie there?"

"Hello?" Callie answered the phone.

"Go get in bed, and I'll be home in a minute. I'll finish tucking you in when I get there."

"Okay. See you soon," she said before hanging up.

Tabby went back over to her friends and sighed. "I'm sorry, ladies, but I have to head out. Crisis at home."

"What?" Ginger and Sally asked in unison. They stopped dancing and turned to Tabby.

"It's what happens when you're a mom. I'm sorry. I had a blast, though. I'll see you all at work." She waved and then hurried out of the club. She fished her keys out of her pocket and didn't stop running until she reached her car.

The conversation with Drew had her bothered. If she

couldn't rely on him taking care of the girls for a few hours, then what *could* she count on? She knew now she shouldn't have thought she'd be able to go out and have fun without any hitches.

She turned the key, and her car made a noise, then died. She tried again, but nothing happened. *This cannot be happening right now.* She tried one more time for good measure. Still, the car didn't start. She slumped forward and shook her head. Could anything else go wrong?

A light tap sounded on Tabby's window, making her sit up. It was Jenni. She turned away and wiped the tears away that had escaped her eyes. She then rolled down her window and looked up at Jenni's concerned gaze.

"Are you all right?" Jenni asked.

There was nothing all right with how Tabby was feeling. She had so many thoughts running through her mind, but no words would come out. She finally looked up and gave a slight smile.

"Car won't start."

"I kind of figured that," Jenni said. "If you need a ride somewhere, I wouldn't mind taking you."

It was like an answer to an unasked prayer. "I don't think I could ask that of you. Are you even ready to go? It's still so early."

Jenni shrugged. "I'm good to go if you need to get out of here. You can call a tow truck for your vehicle."

"Are you sure?" Tabby pressed.

"Absolutely. I'm parked over there." She motioned toward the red Camaro that was only two aisles from hers. Tabby got out of her car, locked it, and followed Jenni. She looked back at the club's entrance to ensure that none of her coworkers had walked out. She didn't want this to get out and for people to talk. When they reached the car, the lights flashed, and Tabby opened the passenger door.

"Thank you for this," Tabby said, getting in.

Jenni got in from the driver's side and inserted her key into the ignition. "Don't mention it. It's the least I could do, especially since you put your nursing skills to good use when you gave me those pills." Jenni lightly touched Tabby's knee in gratitude. Warmth radiated up Tabby's leg, and she was sad when Jenni withdrew her hand.

Tabby looked out the window with a smile. "I graduated with top honors for how well I open medicine cabinets and find over-the-counter pills," she said sarcastically.

Jenni laughed. "It's the little things. What's your address?"

Tabby gave it, and Jenni put it into her GPS. As Jenni pulled out of the parking lot and headed to the house, silence filled the air. Tabby looked at the place on her knee that Jenni had touched. It was an awkward situation to be in, and the lack of conversation left her feeling even stranger.

It was Jenni who spoke first, breaking the silence. "I have a confession," she said.

"Oh yeah?" Tabby turned to look at her. Jenni nodded.

"I saw you were rushing out of the club, and I was curious, so I rushed out after you."

Tabby shook her head. "What about the person you left at the table? Was she your date?"

"Oh, no," Jenni said, laughing. "She's my BFF. We've been best friends for longer than you've been alive."

Tabby didn't know why she was relieved to hear that Jenni hadn't been on a date. She looked at Jenni, whose eyes had lit up when talking about her friend. Jenni said, "But she's only passing through. She lives in Cali, and I was going to see her for a few hours. That's all. I'll text her and tell her what happened."

Jenni made a turn, then continued. "It used to be that when we got together, it was like no time had passed. Tonight felt strange. Like maybe we were drifting apart or something."

"I don't know that BFFs can drift apart like that. I mean, maybe there's something you're both going through, but I feel a friendship like that is always worth salvaging. Don't you?"

Jenni's lips curved into a smile as they made eye contact. "I absolutely do. This is also why I know she'll forgive me for rushing out like that. I'll just say that I had a friend in need. Who can object to that?"

Tabby turned and looked back out the window. That was a good excuse, as far as excuses were concerned. Yet, as far as she knew, she couldn't classify Jenni as a friend. They didn't know one another all that well. Besides, Jenni was out of Tabby's reach when it came to stature and power.

"So, what about your BFF?" Jenni continued.

The question brought a crease between Tabby's eyes as she thought about that. If she was honest with herself, she had lost contact with all her friends once she had gotten married. Sure, she had made new friendships at the hospital when she started working there, but no one she would consider a best friend. She had always said that Drew was her best friend. Now, she laughed when she thought about that. They were more like roommates now—strangers, even.

"I guess I would say my husband," Tabby concluded, hating how pathetic that sounded. Her best friend couldn't be her husband when she was the one who had to rush home to ensure her children were okay because he was too busy being selfish.

"That's sweet," Jenni said. "Believe me, I understand that. In many ways, my wife and I…" Her words trailed off, and the two of them resumed sitting in awkward silence. Tabby turned to Jenni, wanting her to continue and talk about her wife. It was the first time she was getting a deep, introspective look at the woman next to her. Hanna had mentioned a deceased spouse, and now Tabby was intrigued.

"We're here," Jenni said, pulling up to the curb.

"Oh." Tabby turned and looked out the car window. Sure enough, her house stood in front of them. "Thank you again for getting me home. I appreciate it."

Jenni gave a soft smile. "No problem. I hope everything works out."

Tabby started to get out of the car and then hesitated. She had an urge to touch Jenni, and couldn't stop herself from lightly placing her hand on Jenni's, which was on the steering wheel. Jenni's eyes shot to hers. "I heard about your wife," Tabby said. "I can't imagine what you've been through."

Jenni looked surprised and nodded slightly, remaining silent as Tabby finally got out of the car. She ran up to the door, and at the front porch, she turned and waved to Jenni, who waved back before driving off. Tabby lingered a moment, touched by how quickly Jenni had come to her rescue. Jenni always seemed to be doing that. She seemed to genuinely care about Tabby and her family, and that was touching. It was getting harder and harder not to think about Jenni, who was slowly working her way into Tabby's life.

Steadying herself, Tabby entered the house. At first, silence hit her, but then she heard Drew's guitar. She hurried up the stairs to Callie's room. She opened the door and tiptoed inside to see Callie lying in bed, sleeping soundly. She backed out of the room and shut the door behind her.

She then went to Brittany's room. Her elder daughter was asleep as well. She headed back into the hallway and heaved a sigh of relief before going back down the stairs and entering Drew's music room.

He looked up, surprised. "You're home? I wasn't expecting you until midnight or after."

Tabby slumped down on the couch and shook her head. "Are you kidding me? It sounded like you and Callie weren't getting along. She wanted me here."

"But she's in bed, isn't she?"

Tabby released a breath. "She is, but when I talked to you, you acted like I should be ashamed of myself. I needed *one* night out, away, to have some time for myself, and you acted like that was an issue. But then the other night you went out and did whatever you wanted. You still haven't told me where you were or what you were doing. Is that fair?"

"You're being dramatic," he said as he went back to strumming his guitar.

"Dramatic. Okay. Guess I'm just paranoid or too sentimental. Whatever." Tabby stood up and was walking away when the music stopped again.

"What do you want from me?"

Tabby spun on her heel and stared at him. "That's what you have to say? What do I want from you?" She shook her head. "I want us to have a marriage that counts. I want us to be able to tell each other anything. I want my best friend back."

Drew looked down at his guitar, silent. There was her answer. Tabby felt a tear slip down her cheek. She wiped it away and turned to him. "My car is broken down at the club. I'll need to get it towed somewhere."

"Something else to care of," he mumbled.

Tabby sighed. "I'll handle it." She left the music room and was going to head up the stairs when she hesitated and chose a different route. She went through the kitchen and stepped out onto the back porch. She sat down on the chair that looked out to their backyard. The tears wouldn't stop as she tried to move her thoughts from Drew to something more positive. Yet, no matter how hard she tried, she had difficulty remembering anything but the condescending look Drew gave her. She had nearly lost hope for any reconciliation and just needed the strength to get through it all.

CHAPTER EIGHT

Jenni

J enni looked at the clock on the wall. They had been in the room for an hour and all she could deduce was that there was a lot of bickering and arguing going on. She rubbed her temples and silently urged for one of two things to happen. Either get a major migraine that forced her out of there, or keep the migraine away because she didn't want to barf all over the boardroom table.

"Twenty people?" Dr. Gregory O'Shea asked. "That's a lot of employees. Nurses *and* receptionists? How are we going to handle the layoffs?"

"We'll figure it out. The others will have more hours, for sure," Brian, the CEO, spoke up. "But I know there are many employees who would love to have some extra income."

"It sounds like we're just shifting from one employee to the next," Judith Crosby, a nurse practitioner, spoke up, shaking her head. "How does that help Capmed?"

"In the end," Brian stated, "we'll have employees who make less money employed here, which would save the hospital money."

"That's a crock," Dr. Ivan Wesley spoke up. "As I see it here, we're laying off many nurses in the ER. What are we supposed to do without nurses, tell the patients that no one can take care of them? Do you see how that makes no sense whatsoever?"

"You're not looking at the big picture," Brian replied. "Once renovations are done, we can hire some of these people back. Or we can hire new candidates."

"Who start at the bottom of the barrel," Ivan replied. "Is that it?"

Jenni looked over at Charles. He hadn't once spoken at all during the meeting, but she was sure he had some ideas of his own running through that mind of his. He didn't want to risk losing cardiology nurses. He sat back and listened, observing it all. Much like Jenni was doing.

"And there's no other way?" Dr. Regina Masterson asked. "You can't figure any way to save these jobs? And you're saying *twenty* is really the starting point. By the end of it, who's to say how many people actually end up being terminated. Is that correct?"

Brian looked around the boardroom. You could have heard a pin drop. Jenni waited to see exactly what he would say. Her migraine was on the verge of emerging and she braced herself, reaching up to massage her temples once more.

"I have looked at many avenues. I assure you, the board did not decide this lightly."

"What about you, Jenni?" Jenni shifted her gaze to Ivan. "How do you feel about this? After all, your money goes to the hospital, and you're okay with terminating twenty of its senior staff?"

Jenni swallowed and cringed as her headache quickly rushed to her forehead. No, she wasn't okay with it, but what could she do about it? "I wish there were another way," she began. "I have thought about offering up more money, but I don't want to be tapped out, especially if we're looking at Capmed's expansion. I have concluded that my realm of knowledge doesn't go far when it comes to HR."

"And believe me," Pamela Hobson from the HR department spoke up. "If we could find any other option, we would take it."

There was some more grumbling around the table, and Jenni grabbed a small container, which contained two pills, from her pocket. She popped the pills in her mouth, then took a swig of water. She should have done that first thing in the morning, but who would have known how troublesome the meeting would have gotten?

"I vote we take a recess until next week," Brian stated. "At that time, we'll see if anyone can bring some ideas to this meeting that are worth listening to. Meeting adjourned." Jenni jumped up and left the room but waited outside for Charles so that she could discuss the meeting with him.

"What do you think?" she asked.

He shook his head and led the way to the elevator. "Twenty employees are no joke. More than half will be nurses,

If I lose some of my staff, I don't know what I'll do. The cardiology department could be in danger of closing down. I don't see how this is beneficial. They need to realize that we'll lose business." He stepped into the elevator and pressed a button. "But I guess we'll see."

Jenni pressed the button for the main floor. "I think if we all put our heads together, we can figure out a way to salvage these jobs."

"I sure hope so." The doors opened, and he stepped out, but reached his hand back in to stop the elevator from going down. "Cecilia wanted me to invite you to dinner. When are you free?"

"Whenever." She smirked and jokingly corrected, "I mean, my social calendar is *super* busy. You'd better text me a list of dates and I'll get back to you."

He smiled. "Friday night?"

"What do you know? I'm free."

"Great! Come by at sixish and we'll see you then." He waved as the doors closed.

Jenni took the remaining two floors down to the cafeteria. She had gotten her pills in her, but she needed to do the same with food. She stepped into the cafeteria and headed to the seafood counter, grabbed her food and drink, then paid for it and exited through the patio doors to find a seat outside. She found a nice, secluded spot and started to eat.

Jenni didn't mind eating alone. It was something she had grown accustomed to, but as the surrounding tables filled up with friends, she caught herself watching each one and wondering what a difference it would be to have someone sit with her and provide some good company. She took a bite of her seafood salad and kept her eyes lowered to her plate, but she could only look at her food for so long before it made her feel even lonelier, not to mention pathetic. She took a sip of her water and looked up.

Tabby stepped out onto the patio, food in hand. There wasn't an empty table out there, so when Tabby looked in her direction, Jenni motioned for her to come over and join her.

"Are you following me?" Jenni teased.

Tabby's cheeks were bright red. She quickly shook her head. "I swear it's just a coincidence that we always seem to be running into one another. I can find another table to sit at, though."

"What? I was only teasing, Tabby. Sit down. Besides, I would rather have someone here than pretend it isn't awkward being the only person with no one sitting with them. You're doing me a favor."

"In that case," Tabby said, sitting down, "I agree with you. It's awkward eating alone."

Jenni smiled and took a bite of her salad. "I'm glad we ran into one another, though."

"You are?" Tabby asked. "Maybe you're the one who's following me."

Jenni opened her mouth and Tabby laughed. Jenni snapped her mouth shut, glad to see that Tabby was teasing her back.

"Anyway, were you able to get your car fixed?"

"Ahh, yes. I was, thank you. And thanks again for taking me home. It was really nice of you."

Jenni shook her head. "Right place, right time."

"But your friend..." Tabby's voice waned, and Jenni laughed.

"We're still friends. No need to worry about that."

Undoubtedly, Kim had been confused by the sudden way Jenni had left the club, but she had called her BFF later that night and explained the issue, and Kim had accepted it. They would get together before another year could come between them, and she was glad she was able to get Tabby safely home. Deep down Jenni wondered why Tabby had so quickly fled to her house after touching her hand the way she did. Jenni hadn't known how to react when Tabby had offered so much empathy for her wife. It only made her feelings for Tabby deepen.

"What are you eating?" Tabby asked, pointing. "That seaweed sort of thingy."

Jenni snapped out of her thoughts, taking another bite. "It's not so bad. You should try it sometime. Wendy introduced me to this type of food. Never thought I'd ever choose it over a burger and fries." She shrugged. "She surprised me, though, and I've been eating it ever since."

"Wendy?" Tabby asked.

It hit Jenni that she had said Wendy's name for the first time. "My wife," she explained. "The one who passed. She was the health nut in the relationship."

"How did she pass?" Tabby asked softly.

"Drunk driver." Jenni looked down at her salad.

"You don't have to talk about it if you don't want to. I shouldn't have pried."

Jenni looked up. Just having someone interested enough in hearing about Wendy made her feel good. She never used to want to talk about her or bring her up in conversation, but it wasn't because she didn't like talking about her. She knew talking about her in the past tense would mean Wendy was definitely gone.

"She was always trying to get me to work out—something I frowned upon. Then she introduced me to seafood, and it suddenly became something that I craved. Who would have thought? This is a shrimp and tuna salad with a bit of broccoli. Do you want to try it?"

Tabby made a face, then shook her head. "Thanks, but I'll stick to my burger and fries."

Jenni snickered and continued eating. "Tell me about your husband. What's his name? What does he do?"

Tabby dropped her gaze to her plate of food and Jenni worried she had made a grave mistake in asking. "Drew," Tabby finally replied. "He's a musician. Or trying to be. The fact is, he doesn't get many gigs. He has one coming up at a family-friendly venue, but that's only because a friend of a friend got it for him." She smiled, but it was clearly forced. Her eyes were so dim that they startled Jenni.

"Is he good?" Jenni asked.

"Define *good*. I mean, I think he's good. He used to be great. I think over the years he lost confidence, so that hasn't helped his self-esteem when it comes to his playing. He's good enough to get people to listen, but that doesn't necessarily mean he should do it as his full-time job. Does that make any sense?"

"Makes perfect sense. Just because you're good at something doesn't mean you shouldn't do something else to bring home the bucks."

"Yes, and lately..."

When Tabby didn't finish her thought, Jenni touched her hand. "What is it?"

She thought Tabby might brush the sudden touch away, but she didn't. Jenni's pulse quickened.

"Lately," Tabby continued, "I don't know what's happening in our marriage. He says he loves our girls, but he's not pulling his weight. Paying the bills is put on my shoulders because he's always 'trying' to get more gigs. And he's always so angry and bitter. We barely talk, and when we do, it always ends in a fight." Her eyes became misty, and she looked away. "To be honest, I'm a bit lost. I'm not happy and not sure we're still in love. But it's scary to think about ending things."

She wiped her eyes and forced a smile. "Sorry for venting."

Jenni squeezed her hand. "Don't apologize. I'm always here to listen."

The two women gazed at each other and something unspoken passed between them. While it thrilled Jenni, Tabby shifted and looked down, pulling her hand from Jenni's.

Jenni wanted to dig deeper and see why Tabby had pulled away. Still, for now, she was just glad to have Tabby finally open up to her.

⚜

Jenni took a sip of her wine and put it down on the coaster. She sat back in her seat and tried to see if she could hear Charles or Cecilia talking to their kids as they tucked them into bed. There was nothing but silence. She guessed that was a good thing, since she felt awkward trying to eavesdrop on their family time. It'd only been fifteen minutes since they took the kids upstairs, temporarily leaving her alone in the living room.

She checked her watch. It was still early, or she would have said her goodbyes and headed home. But going home to an empty house seemed less appealing than it did most nights, so she didn't bolt out of Charles's home. She leaned forward and picked up her glass once more to take a drink. As she did, she spotted a flyer on the coffee table and picked it up. Drew Brickly, Guitar Soloist. A can't-miss concert! She scanned her eyes over the flyer, and when she heard footsteps on the stairs, she dropped it onto the table and took another drink.

"Wifey is finishing getting them to bed," Charles said, coming into the living room to take a seat. Jenni looked up and smiled, then glanced down at the flier.

"What's that?" she asked nonchalantly, pointing to the flier.

He grabbed it and smirked. "Tabitha," he said, then looked up and met her gaze. "She's the one that you found quite appealing, right?"

Jenni looked away from him. "You said that, not me." She took a sip.

He chuckled. "Right. Anyway, her husband is performing at this show tomorrow night. It's family friendly, so she asked if we wanted to come."

"Are you going to?" Jenni asked, looking up.

He dropped the paper to the table and shrugged. "We talked about it, but we're not sure. You should go. She was asking a bunch of people around the hospital."

"I don't know," Jenni replied. "You don't think that'd be

odd? I mean, I don't really know him or anything. I barely know her."

"Nah, it's open to the public." He shrugged. "You should consider it."

Jenni already *had* considered it, and she was worried that if she showed up, Tabby would think she was stalking her. But she couldn't say that, not in front of Charles.

"We'll see," she said, leaving it at that. Cecilia came down the stairs and heaved a sigh as she entered the living room.

"Tonight was exhausting. Probably because they didn't want to go to bed while their Auntie Jenni was here."

Jenni smiled. "Your kids are so precious."

She was glad to have Cecilia there so that she didn't have to talk about Tabby's husband's band, or Tabby, for that matter. She did find herself curious about the band. Tabby said her husband was good. If she did go, that would be a reasonable excuse, right?

Still, it wouldn't be a good idea. It was best just to forget it. No need to put herself in an awkward situation, especially if she ran into Tabby at the concert. She definitely shouldn't go.

But even as she tried to convince herself, she knew her heart was set on going. She was too curious to see what kind of a man and musician Tabby's husband was, and she liked the idea of "bumping" into Tabby there.

"I think she's zoned out, dear," Cecilia said, breaking Jenni from her thoughts.

"What?" she asked, turning to face Charles's wife.

Cecilia laughed. "I was just being nosy, but you looked like you were lost in your own mountain of thoughts. Or just didn't want to answer my question."

"Most likely both," Charles chuckled. "Can I get you ladies some coffee?"

Jenni nodded. She had been drinking wine most of the night, and if she planned on leaving any time soon, she needed to do something to get the wine out of her system.

He left the living room and went to prepare some coffee, and Jenni glanced over at Cecilia. "So, you were saying?"

Cecilia had a sweet smile on her lips. That was one thing that drew her to the Richards household. Even though Charles was a top cardiologist in the Chicago area, if not the entire Midwest, he and his wife were down-to-earth people. She felt welcome being around them.

"I was just inquiring if there was any lady that had caught your attention recently." Cecilia tilted her head. "Of course, you don't need to answer. I'm just curious. You deserve someone who will make you happy."

"I don't mind, Cecilia. I guess it would be nice to have this conversation with a woman who wouldn't judge me. There is someone…" Jenni's words trailed off. Tabby was married, so it was ridiculous to even think of pursuing her, yet she also couldn't ignore what Tabby had shared with her about feeling lost and unhappy in her marriage. Did that leave an opportunity for Jenni to fill the void? "While Charles isn't here, do you mind if I let this out?"

"Of course not. Please continue."

"As you know, it's been five years since Wendy passed away. In my heart, I know that's enough time for me to move on. Part of me feels ready, but there's still something nagging inside of me. What if I open myself up to love someone and ultimately get my heart broken? And there's the question about age. I'm substantially older than this woman, so should that determine whether I go for it?"

And the fact that she's married should probably come into play, right? She bit her tongue.

"It does seem like this woman has been occupying your thoughts. I can see it in your eyes; you like her." Jenni blushed and looked down as Cecilia continued. "I think it's great. I mean, I have seen you struggling with your wife's death, and to think that you feel you might be ready to open yourself up is truly a step in the right direction. As for the possibility of your heart getting broken, you can't worry about that. If you feel this woman is worth it, then you should absolutely put your heart out there."

"And the age thing?"

"What's a few years' age difference?" Cecilia asked.

"More like fifteen," Jenni said, then grabbed her glass and downed the last of her wine.

"What's fifteen years? I say you have to do what your heart is telling you to do. Don't listen to your head, because it screws you up."

It *was* what Jenni wanted to do, but she also wasn't trying to be a homewrecker. Of course, the decision was ultimately Tabby's, but maybe it was time Jenni made her interests clearer. Did she and Tabby have a chance at love?

"There's one more thing," Jenni began. "She's married."

Cecilia's eyebrows shot up and she opened her mouth to respond, when Charles returned.

He held up the tray of coffee. "Coffee is served."

Jenni released a breath. Hopefully, Charles hadn't heard their conversation and she could keep this minute detail to herself. What Cecilia said did make sense. It was something Jenni had always strived to do: keep her heart open and follow where it led her. She never planned to confess her feelings to a married woman, but she also never planned on falling for Tabby. Now it was just about figuring out the right place and time to tell her.

❧

The crowd was packed, as over two hundred people stood outside waiting for the concert to start. It was in a field near a bar and grill, where you could go inside for shelter if it rained. Jenni looked up at the sky, which had already grown quite dark, and she wasn't so sure she wouldn't be forced to run inside with the rest of the concertgoers.

Jenni stood in the back, mainly out of the way so she could hopefully go unseen. A crack of thunder sounded, and Jenni looked up at the sky again, bracing herself for the downpour that the weatherman had called for. "Just hold off until his set is over," she pleaded to the sky.

She wasn't sure why she was there, other than she wanted to get a feel for the man who had said I do to Tabby. She had the pleasure of meeting their kids and knew they were great, so she hoped to find a man up on the stage who didn't deserve the love of Tabby. It would make her feel better about having feelings for a married woman if Drew wasn't a good guy. Another crack of thunder sounded, and she shivered, not sure she would get the chance to see Drew perform.

"You did decide to come." Jenni whirled around and saw Charles, his wife, and their two kids.

"Auntie Jenni," his daughter Lesa squealed, throwing her arms around her.

"Hey, there. Glad to see you all again," she said, looking at Charles and Cecilia.

"Good to see you," Cecilia replied, pulling Jenni into a hug. "There's a large crowd," she said, parting from the embrace.

"The concert is rain or shine," Charles said. "Hopefully it won't pour until the performance is over." Jenni nodded and turned to the stage.

"Daddy, let's go up here," Noah, Charles's son, insisted, grabbing his father's hand and pulling him closer to the stage.

"Are you coming?" Charles asked, peering over his shoulder.

Jenni smiled and shook her head. "I'm good back here. Might have to cut out early. I'll see you all later." She waved and was grateful they didn't argue. The last thing she wanted was for Tabby to find out she was there. That would bring up too many questions she didn't want to answer. Although, there were a lot of people there, so it wasn't like she couldn't just go with the "I just wanted to enjoy a concert" story.

The music started, and a man came onto the stage. The crowd cheered, so Jenni joined in. "Hello, ladies and gentlemen. My name is Drew Brickly. Thank you for coming out to my first show after a long hiatus. It's good to be back."

As Drew performed, the audience continued to cheer for him. Jenni scanned her eyes around the crowd until she spotted Tabby and her two kids. They were all clapping, but Jenni saw how Tabby's happiness didn't quite shine through her smile and didn't reach her eyes.

I just want to see Tabby happy. The way she smiles around me and how she looks now are like night and day. Am I wrong for thinking we might have a future together? Jenni took a few minutes to get into the music, and she realized how good Drew truly was. She had initially shown up to find evidence that she had every right to go after a married woman, but as the band played, things slowly shifted. She just relaxed and clapped to the music along with the rest of the crowd.

She didn't see anyone from the hospital other than Charles and his family, and it was nice to be unnoticed while she stood in the back. The sound of thunder cracked and a few rain-drops fell, but no one left.

As she watched Tabby and her two girls, she felt a twinge of regret for all of her thoughts about Tabby and Drew split-ting up. That would be hard on their girls, and even if Tabby wasn't happy, she probably didn't want a divorce. What had Jenni been thinking by coming here?

Just one more song. One more song and she would leave and forget this silly notion about going after Tabby. When the song ended, the crowd jumped up and cheered for Drew.

"Thank you! Thank you! You're all wonderful, sticking out the rain with me and the band. Let me introduce everyone. On keyboards you have Joel Hathaway." The crowd cheered, and he went through the rest of the members, then turned back to the crowd. "As I mentioned at the start, I'm Drew Brickly, and I wouldn't be here if it wasn't for three amazing people in my life. I'd like to bring them up on the stage right now. Baby, come on up here."

Jenni, along with everyone else, looked toward where he pointed. Sure enough, he was pointing at Tabby and the two kids. They walked up on stage, and Drew turned to Tabby. "I haven't always been the best husband to you," he said. "But after tonight, I promise you that I'm going to change all that. I love you." He pulled Tabby into his arms and kissed her.

Jenni's jaw dropped. In that one moment, Jenni had gotten all her answers. She shouldn't confess her feelings. She didn't want to put Tabby in a stressful situation. It was better to remain friends and colleagues only. Jenni turned and walked away.

CHAPTER NINE

Tabby

A s the kiss ended, Tabby looked up at Drew. He gave her a huge smile, and the crowd cheered wildly. Tabby turned to the audience and squinted through the rain. Was that Jenni walking away from the crowd? She shook her head. She was probably just imagining it.

"This is my beautiful wife, Tabby," Drew continued. "And these are our beautiful children, Brittany and Callie." The crowd continued to cheer, and the rain fell around them even harder. "I'll tell you what, folks. You've all been so great, I'm going to perform one more song. Darling..." He motioned to the stage exit and Tabby, Brittany, and Callie headed off the stage. As Tabby descended the steps, she spotted Charles and his family.

"Thank you for coming!" she said.

He nodded. "Your husband has an amazing talent."

She smiled, not sure how to respond. She had no credit to take when it came to Drew's talent. She went back to the spot where they had stood before Drew had awkwardly called them on stage. She had been completely blindsided. She had to go up there and be the doting wife, or how would that look? The rain continued but Drew didn't let that stop them. They were under a canopy that was waterproof and kept the instruments safe. He did seem to be in his element, and it reminded her greatly of how he performed when they first got together.

It was emotional, even. She wiped a tear from her eye. The last song he played, titled *You Lift Me*, he had written for her when they had first started dating. A tear slid down her cheek and Brittany wrapped her arm around Tabby's waist. She looked down and Brittany gave her a soft smile. She kissed the top of her head, grateful for her daughter's support. The song ended, and the crowd applauded. She joined in, even cheering Drew as he walked off the stage.

People put their umbrellas up, shielding themselves from the rain, and Tabby did the same. She looked around, waiting to find Drew. After a moment, she spotted him off to the side. He was talking to a blonde woman who was dressed in very little clothing. She was leaning into him, trying to stay out of the rain.

Tabby stayed back until the woman walked away and left Drew alone. "Let's say goodbye to your dad," Tabby said. "I need to get you girls home to bed."

Callie groaned. "Do you?"

Tabby arched an eyebrow. "You know the deal. I said you needed to get home right after the show. That's why we drove separately." Both girls nodded, and they walked over to where

Drew stood talking to the band. "We're gonna head out. I know you have autographs to sign or something."

Drew grabbed a towel and dried his hair as they stood under a canopy tent. "All right, babe," he said. He wrapped his arm around her waist and pulled her to him—possibly something that he was doing for show. He kissed her hard, with all eyes on them. Tabby played along since avoiding the kiss would have looked bad in front of the crowd.

"I'll try not to be too late. Don't miss me." He winked at Tabby, who gave a weak smile. How could they pretend like everything was all right? She wasn't the type to forgive and forget.

The three of them turned and left through a back alley to get to their car. When they reached the car and were inside, Callie spoke up. "Dad is great, right?"

Tabby looked over her shoulder to her daughter, who was in the backseat. "Your dad is one of the best," she said. When she turned back around, she noticed that Brittany's brows were furrowed. Tabby reached across the seat to touch her daughter's hand. Drew's sudden change was confusing for her, so it must be even more confusing for their thirteen-year-old.

She pulled out of the spot and headed home. If Drew was sincere, that was one thing, but how could she trust any honesty coming from him? There had been too much deceit in their marriage to think that he was suddenly going to turn a corner. She didn't buy it.

When they pulled up to their house, Callie was sound asleep in the backseat. "Callie?" Tabby whispered, shaking her lightly.

Callie groaned, then turned and opened her eyes. "Are we

there yet?" she mumbled, stretching out and sitting up in her booster seat.

"Yep. We're here. Brittany is already upstairs getting washed up for bed." She helped Callie out of the car, and they went inside and headed upstairs.

"Mom?" Callie asked.

"Yes?"

"When Dad gets home will you ask him to come upstairs and tuck me in?" She turned to look at Tabby as they reached Callie's bedroom. Tabby nodded and Callie pushed open her door.

"I'll be in in a minute to check on you." Thunder cracked from outside, shaking the whole house. Callie's eyes bugged out. "And read you a story for bed. There's nothing to fear, Peaches."

"Except fear itself," Callie replied.

"That's right." She pulled Callie into her arms, holding her tightly. "Now, go get cleaned up, and I'll be in soon."

Callie went in to grab her things as Tabby walked to Brittany's room. She knocked, then opened the door. Brittany sat on the edge of her bed, her head down as she clutched a stuffed teddy bear in her arms. For a moment, she looked like a toddler again, and Tabby's heart melted. Tabby walked in and sat in the seat next to her. When Brittany looked up, she was crying.

"What's wrong, sweet girl?" Tabby asked, brushing a couple of tears from her eyes.

"Tonight was like it used to be. Like I remembered it. But..." Her words trailed off. Tabby pulled her into her arms.

"It's going to be okay. I promise you. We're all going to be okay," Tabby said, stroking Brittany's hair.

As Tabby continued to soothe her daughter, she feared that was one promise she wouldn't be able to keep. She didn't want her children pulled into this, but that was exactly what was bound to happen.

"Shhhh," Tabby whispered. "Everything is going to be just fine."

❧ ⠿⠿⠿ ⠿⠿⠿ ❧

The light flicked on in their bedroom. Tabby opened her eyes and turned to the door as Drew wandered into the room. He stumbled over to the bed and leaned on her. Immediately, she smelled Coke and Jack Daniels on his breath.

"What time is it?" she whispered, looking over to the clock. "Three o'clock?" She reached up to push him off of her. "Where have you been?"

"Baby, I need you," he said. "Shhhhhhh." He grabbed Tabby's wrist and pulled her to him, kissing her hard on the lips.

"No," she groaned, pushing him off her. "Talk to me." She pushed him back.

"Talk to you? I don't want to talk. I want to have sex. Don't deprive your husband." He straddled her as he pushed her down on the bed and tried to kiss her again. He grabbed her T-shirt and tugged on it.

"I said no!" She pressed her fists hard against his chest, pushing him until he fell off the bed.

"Are you kidding me?" he yelled, stumbling to his feet.

"You're drunk," she said, scooting off the bed. "How'd you get home?"

"Cab." He shrugged. "I'll get my car tomorrow. What's the big deal? We're *married*. And with the way I introduced you tonight, I assumed I'd have you like putty in my hands."

Tabby's jaw dropped. Putty in his hands? Who did he think he was messing with? She wasn't about to have sex with him because he was portraying himself as a caring husband.

"What was that? Trying to get good points with your boys? Trying to get people to think you're a great guy? Well, you might have fooled them, but you sure as hell didn't fool me. You got that?"

She hurried toward the door, but he beat her to it, blocking Tabby from leaving. "What are you going to do? Force me to have sex with you? You might be going through some changes, changes that I don't even understand, but you would never force me into doing something I didn't want to do. This isn't working and you know it."

Drew's eyes dropped down to the floor, and for a brief moment, Tabby saw sorrow in his gaze. When he looked up, his drunken eyes had softened, and he stepped aside. "I'm sorry," he mumbled.

She nodded and was reaching for the door handle when he spoke again. "They hired me on to do two more weeks of shows. Adults only. It'll be at a different venue this time—a club. We'll have some more money coming in. I guess I got carried away with the celebration."

Tabby hesitated and looked over at him. What bothered her the most was that she knew the man Drew was, and that man was not the same person standing before her now. She wanted to be happy for him. Deep down, she was, but her heart was shattered in so many ways that it was hard to hold on to.

"Congratulations, Drew," she quietly replied before walking out and going down the hall to the spare room. She escaped inside and closed the door behind her, then fell to her knees, her head down. There wasn't a way of getting past this. It was time to make some serious decisions, and that meant saying goodbye to the way her life had been the past twelve years.

CHAPTER TEN

Jenni

J enni was eating lunch at the hospital. She took a bite of her burger and looked over the budget that she had spread out on the table. She stared at the money going out, comparing it to what came in. If she could swing a bit more funding, then maybe they would drop the horrible idea of firing people. It would be a struggle, but it was possibly worth it. She sipped on her Diet Coke as she stared at the numbers.

"What are you staring at so intensely?"

She looked up and saw Hanna standing there, leaning over to see the paperwork. "Nothing!" Jenni said, flipping the papers over. It was important to her that no one got wind of what was going on until they finalized the details.

"Clearly looks important," Hanna replied, laughing. "Mind if I sit here? I hate sitting by myself."

"Nope. Have at it." Jenni straightened the pile in front of her and pushed it to the side, making some more room. "Don't you usually eat with Tabby or one of the other nurses?" Jenni asked. She cringed when she mentioned Tabby's name, as she didn't want anyone to suspect that she was interested in her.

"Usually. But Sally and Ginger are off today and Tabby had lunch plans with her husband." She shrugged. "They're having a pretty important talk, I assume."

"Oh? How so?" Jenni asked, hoping she sounded nonchalant.

Hanna took a bite of her salad, then shrugged. "I don't know. I don't want to talk smack about her marriage or anything, especially since she's not here to defend it, or him. It's just, I sometimes get the feeling she wishes she had said 'I don't' at the aisle." She shrugged. "But, hey. Some marriages just aren't made to last. Divorce is a popular alternative, or so I hear."

Jenni frowned. She needed to know more. Tabby had told her about her unhappiness, but was she really considering divorce? "They have two kids, right?" Hanna arched an eyebrow. "I ran into them at the grocery store," Jenni explained hastily.

"Yeah," Hanna said, continuing to furrow her eyebrows. "Anyway, just because you have a child doesn't mean it's still all rainbows and kittens. This stays between us, okay?" Jenni nodded, drawn by Hanna's every word. "I've caught Tabby crying in the storage closet. She shrugs it off, but I've worked here long enough to see women who are abused, and some-times I wonder if maybe Tabby is one of those women."

"Abused? Physically?"

"I couldn't say that," Hanna quickly replied. "It wouldn't be fair to go there without having physical proof. But sometimes emotional abuse is even worse—at least, in my opinion. And I could be totally wrong." She dug into her salad as Jenni watched her. "I really shouldn't have said anything. It's not my place, so please don't tell anyone I said this."

Jenni shook her head. "You don't have to worry about me. I won't say anything."

The two sat silently for a few minutes, each lost in their own thoughts. Jenni's mind was all over the place. Maybe everything Drew said at the concert was just for appearances, so that people would think he was a saint—a man who loved his wife and kids and would never harm them, whether physically or emotionally. She popped a fry into her mouth. It was already one of those days when she felt she needed a greasy burger and fries, and now, she realized she needed it even more.

"You've been here a lot lately," Hanna said, changing the subject. "Are you attached to the hospital food that much?"

Jenni smirked and nodded. "Yep. You caught me." She thought about the financial budget that still lay on the table. "I was just thinking that investing money in this place should mean I invest in the employees, too. That's all." She tilted her head. "How many years have you worked here, Hanna? And what's your number one reason you love your job?"

"Twenty-one years. Can you believe it? Sometimes it feels like no time has passed. Other days it feels like I'm living in a never-ending loop." Hanna snickered. "But I do love my job. I would say getting to meet new people is one of my favorite things about it. Are you interviewing staff for the news?" She laughed, taking a bite of her salad.

Jenni listened to the crunch of Hanna's chewing, searching for a reason. "No, but twenty-one years is no joke."

Even though Jenni didn't know yet who was getting terminated first, she knew it was likely that Hanna would be at the top of the list. They were starting with the most senior staff, and Hanna fit right in that bracket.

She dropped her eyes and stared at her food, her stomach dropping. She couldn't eat another bite. It was impossible having to let go of the people that she had gotten to know, even the ones she was newly getting to know. For whoever did get fired, it was going to be a blow to their families.

"I wouldn't do anything else," Hanna admitted quietly. "Capmed has become my life."

She smiled wider as she talked about her job, which bothered Jenni even more. Everyone was getting blindsided. Why couldn't they do this some other way? "I hate to eat and run, but I have to head out," Jenni said, grabbing her tray and snatching up her papers.

"All right. See ya." Hanna waved and Jenni hurried off, dropping her garbage into the trash. She rushed out of the cafeteria and headed straight for Brian's office. His secretary wasn't there. Good. Brian's door was shut, and she pounded on it. She heard a muffled response and opened the door.

Brian looked up. "Jenni! This is a surprise." He started to get up, but she held out her hand.

"Stay seated. This won't take long." She stepped into his office and pleaded her case. "I know that you think going behind everyone's back to terminate employees is the best route, but what if there was another option?"

"Like what?"

"Bring everyone together, sort of like an assembly. Talk to them. Get their insight. You brought the doctors here, but *they* aren't the ones who'll have to worry about losing their job. Prepare these people."

Brian sighed and looked down at his computer, shaking his head. "I know that you're thinking with your heart, and I have always valued your opinion, which is why we invite you to all the board meetings, but I don't want people freaking out. If I tell them that we're terminating employees, those who are safe will start to get nervous. They'll go out and look for other jobs and we don't want to have a mass exit. Do you understand that?"

"Yes," Jenni admitted. "But I also know that I have been in a similar position. I worked at a company that made layoffs. I was blindsided and lost my job. I bounced back, but some of these people might have families and have to support those families. I just think it would be important for them to have notice so that they can be prepared and maybe look for some other options."

"There will be severance packages," Brian stated. "We're not terminating anyone who isn't going to have compensation while they're trying to get back on their feet."

Jenni frowned. "But is that enough?"

He groaned. "Jenni, it probably would never be enough. That's something that we'll have to accept. I will say this, though. I'm doing everything I can to save some of these jobs.

That's why we haven't carried this decision out yet. There are a few things that we're looking into. So don't fret."

She nodded, feeling a bit reassured by his words, and walked to the door. "Thank you for your time." She turned away and started to leave.

"Jenni?" She turned around, waiting for Brian to speak. "At the next board meeting, I'll be passing out a list of people we have to let go. You'll be one of the first to know. If you decide then to prepare someone from that list, or multiple someones, then I won't stop you. Just so you know."

She smiled. "Thank you." She turned away and closed the door behind her. Jenni reached her fingers up and massaged her temples, her migraine slowly working its way back into her head. It was the stress. She knew that, but hopefully soon she would have the knowledge she needed to move forward.

CHAPTER ELEVEN

Tabby

Tabby stared at Drew from across the table as he noisily crunched on his food and then wiped his mouth, barely removing the mayonnaise that was on his lower lip. She looked down at her half-eaten chicken, now cold. It was nearly time to get back to work, and as things stood, she wasn't confident they'd gotten anywhere with their talk.

"So, are you going to support me in my gigs?" Drew asked.

Tabby looked up and stared at him, ready to toss her napkin on her plate and storm out of there. Had he even spent the hour listening to her, or had everything gone in one ear and out the other?

"What?" he asked, chomping down on his sandwich.

"Counseling. Are you for it or against it?"

He smirked. "Do I even need to answer that?"

Her jaw clenched. If Drew wasn't willing to put in the effort, then why should she? It would be one-sided and fail miserably. She was trying here, but Drew didn't seem the least bit interested. She pushed her plate to the edge of the table.

"Are you finished, ma'am?" the waitress asked, approaching them.

She looked up and nodded, then looked across at Drew, waiting for the waitress to leave. "We've done counseling before, and it worked."

"Mostly," he said. "Guess it didn't stick if we have to do it again."

"Not because of my choice," she hissed, glaring at him. "Please tell me you don't see this as all my problem. We don't communicate anymore. I'm trying to fix this."

"We stopped communicating because you stopped coming home at night," he said. "That's not my problem."

"You're right. I was working, and for that, I apologize." She fought the urge to roll her eyes, then heaved a sigh. Arguing with him would only cause more turmoil, and Tabby had decided that working things out for their kids was something she was prepared to do. If she got even an inkling that he was ready for the same, she'd feel a lot better. "If you don't think counseling is something you're willing to put your heart into, then okay. We can separate right now."

His jaw dropped at those words, and Tabby continued to stare him down. His eyes softened a bit, and for just a little while, he looked like the man she had fallen in love with. She felt the tears burning at the back of her eyes and looked away from him. She didn't want to cry, not there, not in front of him, but she was struggling. She lifted a hand to her face and flicked the tears away.

"Don't cry, Tabby Bear," Drew whispered.

She turned back to him, her breath hitching. The last time he had called her that pet name was the night they had conceived Callie. It burned in her memory because it had been so long ago. She opened her mouth, but bit back her words. He reached out and touched her hand.

"I do love you. You know that, right?"

"I think so," she replied softly. She nodded and looked down at his hand as he intertwined their fingers. "And I love you, which is why I want us to get help."

"If it will make you feel better, then we'll do it." His eyes were actually showing concern, and she wanted to believe his every word.

"Thank you Drew." As the words left her, his phone started ringing. He grabbed it from the table and slid his finger across the screen to answer it. "I have to take this. Put the meal on the card." Then he was gone.

Tabby was too shocked to comprehend what had just happened. They were, for once, having a sweet moment. Then suddenly, it was gone, all because of a phone call? He couldn't call the person back? She grabbed some cash from her purse and tossed it down on the table. She didn't have time to wait for the waitress to bring her card back anyway. As it stood, she was already going to be late getting back from lunch. Luckily, the hospital was within walking distance, and she had good shoes on.

She got up from the table, her mind still on the abrupt way Drew left. She walked out of the restaurant and was headed back to the hospital when she paused and reached in her purse, rifling for her phone. She turned to go back to the restaurant when she saw Drew standing against the building, just hidden in an alley. When she drew closer, she could hear whispering. He looked up, and when his eyes met hers, he turned and walked away.

Tabby stared after him. He had definitely seen her. Who was he talking to and why the secrecy? Tabby frowned as she entered the restaurant, walking back to her table and spotting her phone. She grabbed it, relieved, but as soon as she did, her thoughts returned to Drew. *Maybe* you're being paranoid. Maybe he didn't see you.

As Tabby left the restaurant, she looked up and down the alley to see if Drew was still around. When she was certain he had disappeared, she hurried back to the hospital. Worrying about it now wasn't beneficial to anyone, least of all her. She had work to do. Still, it nagged at her, nearly making her crazy as she clocked back in.

She left the breakroom utterly confused, when then the worst-case scenario struck her. What if everything Drew had said to her was a lie, and he was only trying to appease her? What if the person on the other end of the line was a woman that Drew didn't want Tabby to find out about? Tears slowly started down her cheeks as she got in the elevator and pushed for her floor.

You don't even know. Why worry about something that might not even be true? So much disappointment had plagued her over the years that the only plausible excuses seemed to be the right ones. The doors opened, and she stepped off the elevator, her tears no closer to stopping. As she rounded the corner, she spotted Jenni. Their eyes met and Tabby quickly escaped into the storage room. No way was she going to get caught bawling in front of Jenni.

She leaned against the wall, covering her face in her palms.

"Tabby? May I come in?" Jenni's voice sounded through the door, followed by two knocks.

Tabby cleared her throat and desperately looked around for her escape, or at least something to wipe her eyes with. The knocks came again. She groaned and fell back against the wall. There was no use. She had been caught.

Tabby opened the door and Jenni's brows furrowed. "Are you okay?" she asked.

The look on Jenni's face was so concerned and so caring. It was such a contrast to Drew's constant indifference toward her, how he looked through her and was sweet one second only to flip personalities the next. She missed feeling cared for and loved. She missed having a stable relationship.

She flung herself into Jenni's arms, not caring how it looked. Jenni had been such a source of warmth ever since they had met, and the way she felt drawn to her was always in the back of her mind. For a moment, she just wanted to give in. She wanted Jenni to hug her, soothe her, and tell her that everything was okay. That all the conflicted feelings Tabby felt about her attraction to Jenni and her failing marriage would somehow make sense.

Without hesitating, Jenni returned the hug, wrapping her soft arms around Tabby and pulling her into a comforting embrace. "Tell me what's wrong," Jenni said with such tenderness that more tears flooded out of Tabby.

Tabby had reached her breaking point.

<hr />

Jenni listened intently as Tabby spilled everything. From the way her marriage had been slowly crumbling over the years, to the moment she had seen Drew hurrying away from her in that alley. Jenni didn't interrupt, and Tabby was relieved to finally get it all off her chest. She looked up and sighed.

"I didn't mean to blubber that whole story out to you," she said, wiping the tear from her eye. "It just needed to come out, and I guess I didn't realize how much I had to tell someone. I'm sorry, for your sake, that that person was you."

Jenni shook her head. "Give me a minute." She left the closet and Tabby stared awkwardly at the door. Had she scared her off? A moment later, Jenni returned with a box of Kleenex.

"Thank you," Tabby sniffed.

"You don't have to apologize. Not to me. You needed to let this out and I'm glad I was here. I'm sorry that you're going through this," she said, frowning, "but I don't regret you telling me all that." There was a slight pause, and she looked at Tabby. "So he was your best friend, huh?"

Tabby huffed. "Well, he was, at one point. I guess I never wanted to admit that things had gotten so rough, especially not to someone I was just getting to know." Tabby looked down at the floor, suddenly feeling vulnerable. "You must think I'm a real nutcase."

They met each other's eyes, and Jenni quickly shook her head. "I don't. Not at all."

Tabby wanted to believe that, but after spilling her life story to this woman, she worried that she would be seen as less of a woman in front of her. But Jenni seemed to have a kind and honest demeanor, and Tabby let her fears slip away.

"Drew thinks that I should just be his happy wife and support him when he goes out to all these music gigs, but someone has to stay home with the girls. These gigs are at a club, so what does he expect me to do with Callie and Brittany? I *will* support him, by being where our daughters need me. At home." Tabby wiped her eyes and shook her head. "I just never dreamed my marriage would come to this."

"Are your parents around?" Jenni quietly asked, taking a seat on the floor next to Tabby.

"My dad had a heart attack a few years back. We sent him into a nursing home because my mom couldn't take care of him anymore. He died a couple of months later. My mother moved to Florida for her job and she'll probably retire there. We used to be really close. Then I married Drew and, well, things sort of changed."

"She doesn't come around to see her grandchildren?" Jenni asked.

"They FaceTime. But, no, not a whole lot. She just doesn't see eye to eye with Drew on most things. Sadly, I'm now really seeing that, too."

Jenni nodded. "Seems like you have a burden on your shoulders and don't really have the support system to handle it. So, trust me, I don't mind listening."

Tabby smiled. "Thank you." She looked at her watch and

groaned. "And now I'm going to get fired because I was supposed to be back thirty minutes ago."

"I'll handle that," Jenni said, standing to her feet.

Tabby frowned. "What? No. I can take care of it."

Jenni tilted her head. There was a sincerity in her look that made Tabby bite back her argument. "You can't go out there feeling the way you're feeling. Pull yourself together. Put your chin up." She smiled as she pressed her thumb to Tabby's chin and lifted it, and smiled.

Tabby lifted her gaze to meet Jenni's. Despite feeling torn about the possibility that Drew was having an affair, she smiled. Tabby felt compelled to do what Jenni said, because as it stood, Jenni was the only one who seemed supportive of Tabby.

"You got this," Jenni said.

Tabby reached out and touched Jenni's arm before she could leave. Jenni looked over her shoulder and Tabby released a breath. "Please don't tell anyone about this. I mean, my mental breakdown and my marriage problems. I try to hide it, you know?"

Jenni nodded, but as she turned, Tabby reached out for her arm again. "I was going to ask, were you at the concert the other day? I thought I saw you, but when I went searching for you after, you were gone."

Jenni looked away, then shook her head. "Must've been my doppelganger. I had better get back to work myself. I've got you, though." Then she spun on her heel and left the closet.

Tabby leaned back against the wall and stared up at the ceiling. That was strange. She was almost positive she had seen Jenni, but that didn't matter. What mattered now was pulling herself together. She couldn't fathom what Jenni would tell her superiors, but she trusted her. And though she suspected things about Drew, she didn't have any proof. And there was still the possibility that it was all in her mind. Either way, she wanted to get to the bottom of it, once and for all.

CHAPTER TWELVE

Jenni

The conversation with Tabby wouldn't leave her. She didn't know why Tabby felt the need to stick it out with her husband, and surely her daughters would be better off without a toxic marriage playing through their lives.

Still, she could only stand on the sidelines and watch it play out in front of her. It saddened her, but she didn't know what else she could do about it. Still, that didn't stop her from walking into the club that Drew was performing at that Saturday night. She would only stay an hour, tops. At least, that's what she told herself.

As she stood in the back, leaning against a table, a beer in hand, Drew came onto the stage, the band playing behind him. She sipped on her beer and tried not to sway to the music. He was talented, but she was there to be a spy, not enjoy herself. What she was spying for, exactly, she wasn't sure. She just had the feeling she needed to get to know Drew a little bit more to have a real understanding of who the guy was.

"Let me hear you all sing," he yelled out. Jenni looked around. Everyone there seemed to know the song and was singing it right along with him. She then looked back to the stage and really took the time to study Drew. He seemed charismatic and down to earth, and the crowd seemed to love him. She caught herself clapping in time to the music. As the song died, she stopped clapping and shook her head. It was stupid to get too caught up in it. She felt like she was just making a fool out of herself by being there.

She listened to a few more songs, after which the band took a break. She turned around to leave. If she was only going to fall under his spell—more like ruse—then she didn't want any part of it. All marriages had bad spurts, and maybe Tabby and Drew were only going through one of those. If she wanted to help, she needed to give them the respect their marriage deserved.

Before she could leave, though, she spotted Charles and Cecilia. His eyes lit up as he saw her. "Hey there. I didn't know you were going to come back out to another concert. Cool scene, isn't it?"

Jenni forced a smile. It was a scene that was too young for her liking, but then again, Charles was only a few years younger than her. Maybe she had somehow gotten too old. "Just came by for a drink. I didn't even know he was performing." She turned to Charles and Cecilia. "Where are the kiddos?"

"With the babysitter." He wrapped his arm around his wife.

"Out on a date with this beautiful woman. It isn't often that I get to hang out, and we enjoyed the concert the other day, so I thought we would take advantage of one of his gigs. He's a great musician, and there's nothing like showing support for Tabitha." He took a sip of his beer. "Do you want to have a seat and join us?"

"No, but thank you. I was just about to head out." She started to move away from them.

"Nonsense," he said. "It's early. At least have another drink." He got up from his seat. "I'll go get you one. What do you want?"

"You don't have to do that," Jenni argued, "but thanks. I'll go grab my beer." She turned from the table and went to the bar. One more beer and then she'd be out of there.

"What can I get ya?" the man behind the bar asked.

"I'll take a beer—anything you have on tap." Jenni sat down on the stool and waited.

"This seat taken?" She turned to see Drew, of all people, grabbing the stool next to her. He had a smirk on his lips, and she shook her head, then quickly looked away from him. There was a gleam in his eyes the moment she met his gaze. He continued. "It's a beautiful night to stay in, don't you think?" He placed his order, and she frowned, turning to him.

"Meaning?"

"It's starting to storm out there. Reminds me of the last time I performed, at an outdoor venue. I'd definitely say this is a better fit. Wouldn't you?" He took a sip of his beer and their eyes met again. He winked as Jenni grabbed her glass and downed more of the beer than she should have in one gulp.

"Have a good night," Jenni muttered.

He reached out and touched her arm. It was a soft touch that sent the hair on Jenni's arm standing. "Don't rush off. The concert is only in intermission. It will be back for another hour, then maybe after that we can get to know one another better." He winked at her, and she stared back in shock. "Come on. You're sexy, and I saw you watching me from afar. I'm game if you are."

Jenni looked down at his ring finger. His ring wasn't there, but she saw the faint tan line. She looked up and slowly pulled her arm back. "I don't think my girlfriend would like that too much."

He shrugged. "Bring her along. We'll make beautiful music together."

Jenni looked at her drink, considering tossing it straight into his face, then met his sneaky grin. He was a player, and Jenni wondered if Tabby realized that. If he was hitting on her, then chances were that he had hit on several other women along the way. Tabby deserved better than that.

"Not interested," she replied.

He looked surprised, then quickly composed himself. "Babe, that's not usually the response. Are you sure you know what you're saying? Perhaps you're lost in my dazzling smile." He reached out for her wrist, clamping down with his grip. She tugged her arm back, but his grip got tighter.

Jenni latched down on her lower lip, glaring at him as he kept his hand strongly wrapped around her wrist. "Listen here. When a woman says no, she means no. Got that? Let go of my wrist before I knee you where it hurts most." He released her wrist, and she stepped back from him. "Have a great night."

She yanked her hand away, spun on her heel, and hurried to leave.

"Jenni," Charles called out. She had forgotten about Charles and Cecilia. She forced a smile as she glanced in his direction. "Aren't you going to get that drink?"

"Already had it. But I'm starting to get a migraine, so I'm just going to head home. You both enjoy the rest of your date. I'll see you around." She escaped before they could ask any more questions.

She was only a few feet from the door when she heard her name. "Jenni? Is that you?" Jenni jerked her attention to another table, where Hanna and a man sat. Hanna jumped up. "I didn't expect to see you here."

Jenni gave a slight grin and turned to look up at the stage as Drew rejoined the band and started to strum some notes on his guitar. "Just came in for a drink," she lied.

Hanna nodded. "Oh. That's Tabby's husband." Hanna pointed to the stage.

Jenni's jaw dropped. "Oh wow, really? What a coincidence!" Her head started pounding, and she really felt that migraine coming on. "Small world, huh?" She backed up toward the door. "I had best be going. Not feeling the greatest."

"Oh? Take care!" Hanna said, waving and turning back to the guy she was with—probably her husband, Jenni assumed.

Jenni left the club with a sick feeling in her stomach. It was possible that Hanna would tell Tabby she saw her there. She just hoped that Hanna would forget the short encounter and be too engrossed in the man she was with. Otherwise, Jenni was liable to have plenty of explaining to do.

CHAPTER THIRTEEN

Tabby

The sound of light music played over the speakers as Tabby sat at the desk and stared at the computer absentmindedly. She grabbed a pen and started tapping, lightly going along with the music, but then dropped it and rubbed her eyes. If the afternoon was going to continue dragging on this long, she couldn't fathom being stuck there for one more minute. The good thing was that the ER didn't have enough sick patients to occupy the three nurses on duty. The bad thing was that it meant sitting and staring at the computer, hoping for a trauma patient to come in, which wasn't great.

She groaned and stood up from the computer, turning to find Hanna coming out of the supply closet with an armload of supplies tucked in her arms. Tabby hurried over to help, wheeling a cart over and grabbing some items before they fell to the floor.

Hanna snickered. "It's pretty slow when two of the three nurses have to stretch to find things to do. But Sally has it all under control. What are we needed for, eh?"

"Supplies, supplies, and more supplies," Tabby chuckled.

"A nurse's job is never done," Hanna joked as they entered a vacant room.

The quietness of the room settled over them as Tabby and Hanna restocked the supplies. As her mind wandered, Tabby thought of the way Jenni had held her and comforted her at her lowest moment. Though none of her problems were fixed, being with Jenni like that made the weight on her shoulders feel lighter. She smiled softly to herself.

After fifteen minutes of going room to room, Hanna looked over at Tabby. "Did you see Jenni today or something?"

"No, why?"

"Because you're smiling."

Tabby froze. *Strange. How did Hanna know I was smiling because of Jenni?*

Before she could get into it, Hanna switched topics. "Oh, I went and saw Drew last night."

Tabby hesitated, then slid her eyes to Hanna. "Oh yeah? How was it?" she asked nonchalantly.

"Good. He's super talented. I know I've mentioned I thought so before, but he really seems to be in his element when he's performing. And the crowd adores him."

"Yeah, they usually do," Tabby muttered, reaching to the back of the drawer to pull some instruments forward.

"What was that?" Hanna asked.

"Oh, nothing. Glad you enjoyed it."

"Matt and I both did," she said. She looked up and met Tabby's glance. "I know you're a very private person, Tabby, but are things okay at home?"

Tabby quickly looked down at the drawer she was working on. "I don't know what you're getting at. You're pretty private as well. I think it was a few years before I even knew Matt existed." Tabby chuckled to make light of Hanna's question.

Hanna didn't laugh back, so Tabby sighed. "Things can be complicated, but you know that. Marriage isn't for the faint-hearted."

"That is very true. I just want to make sure you know that you have someone here you can chat with if you want. That's all." She gave Tabby a heartwarming smile, which Tabby appreciated, but bringing her home life into the hospital was something Tabby felt she had to steer clear of. Besides, now that she had Jenni to talk to, she didn't have to worry about not having a friend she could confide in.

"What brought this on, anyway? Did you think I was hiding something about my marriage?"

"Well, I sort of expected to see you at Drew's performance last night. When I didn't, I wondered if maybe something was going on at home. There's nothing to be ashamed of, and I'm sorry for assuming. As you said, marriage is tough. Lord knows Matt and I have had our share of issues. We've worked through them, but we also never had kids. We haven't had to share our love and time with a family. It's only the two of us."

"I appreciate your concern, but since we do have kids, someone has to stay home with them. There's nothing more to it than that. Thanks for voicing your concern. No worries, though."

Tabby closed the drawer she had been working on for way too long, and Hanna said, "You're welcome. And if you ever need to talk…"

"I'll know where to turn. Got it. Thank you." They left the room and moved to the last room in the hallway that needed restocking.

"Oh, you know who I saw at the performance?" Hanna asked.

"Who?" Tabby asked, pushing the cart into the room.

"Jenni. I was surprised to see her. She said that she just happened to be at the club. What a coincidence, right?"

Tabby stared down at the cart of supplies that were left to be loaded into the room. It was more than just a coincidence. She had confided in Jenni about Drew and mentioned the club and his upcoming performances. She knew he was going to be there. What was she doing? Spying?

"Tabby?" Hanna asked, breaking into the silence.

"Sure, it's a coincidence, but I'm sure bigger coincidences have happened. That's all she said? That she just happened to be at the club?"

"Yep. I just bumped into her for a few seconds."

"Was she alone?" Tabby inquired.

"I didn't see her with anyone, but as I mentioned, it had happened so fast," Hanna responded, continuing to stock the room.

Tabby wasn't sure how to feel. She didn't want to jump to conclusions, but it was odd that Jenni had gone to see Drew right after she had told Jenni about her suspicions. Jenni had been so kind, but she didn't ask Jenni to help, only listen. It felt like Jenni was overstepping an unspoken boundary by going to check up on Drew behind her back—if that's what she did.

As they worked, Tabby got a call. "It's the hospital," she said.

"Maybe it's an emergency," Hanna replied, dropping her items back into the cart.

"Hello," Tabby answered.

"It's Bianca at the front desk. Jennifer Jennison is here to see you. Are you free?"

"Sure," Tabby replied. "I'll be right there." She pocketed her phone and looked at Heather. "I have a visitor. I'll catch up with you after."

"No problem. I'm almost done anyway."

Tabby quickly left the room and walked down the hallway to meet Jenni. This was good timing, as Tabby wanted to talk to her. She didn't appreciate Jenni going to stalk her husband. What was that going to prove, anyway?

Bianca was waiting on a patient when Tabby reached the desk, and Jenni was leaning against the counter. When Tabby walked around the corner, Jenni looked up and met her eyes, stepping away from the desk.

"We need to talk," Jenni stated.

"You're right. We do," Tabby responded. She grabbed Jenni's arm and pulled her behind her toward the nearest closet. Once inside, she locked the door and turned to stare at Jenni. "I know you went to see Drew perform the other night and it can't be a coincidence. I didn't ask for your help with him."

Jenni's jaw dropped. "I know you didn't ask for my help,

but what about your husband? Don't you want to know the truth?"

"You can't go out stalking my husband. What made you think that it would be a good idea?"

"I wanted to protect you."

Tabby laughed. "Protect me? I don't need your protection. And to find out from Hanna because she saw you there? Luckily, she thinks you just happened to be there, but you and I both know that's not true. This is not okay, Jenni. You should have just minded your own business."

"You deserve better than Drew," Jenni insisted.

Tabby threw up her arms. "That's not for you to say. I shouldn't have trusted you. You betrayed my trust by going to spy on him. What point are you trying to make?" Tabby turned and stepped away, frustrated.

"I know that when I have a friend who's hurting, I try to fix it. Blame me for that—for caring too much. I guess I'm a monster for trying to do the right thing."

Tabby turned on her heel and stared at her. "But it got you nowhere, did it? Brava." Tabby clapped. "It just doesn't make sense that you thought this was the only route you could take."

Jenni stepped closer to her. "It made me see the jerk you're married to."

Tabby snorted. "What did he do? Throw a guitar pick out to a beautiful woman, or wink at her? I know what musician life means. Drew is a musician, and that's how he drew me in. A guitar pick and an eyewink. It's not exactly something he's going to change. I get it, and that's what I signed up for. He comes home to me, and that's what matters."

"You don't really know who your husband is, Tabby. You think he's this guy who's just gotten distant at home and doesn't see how hardworking you are. And barely acknowledges you when he is home. You see him as someone who doesn't listen, but deep down you'll accept that because he's your husband and the father of your children. But what I saw…"

Jenni shook her head, and Tabby frowned. "I saw a man who goes to a club and is grateful you're not there because then he can flirt with all the women he wants behind your back and you'll have no idea. I'm here telling you the truth. Whether you want to listen to me or not, that's totally fine, but he's a cheat, Tabby. Until you realize that, you're liable to screw up your life even further."

"What are you talking about?" Tabby asked, clenching her jaw.

"I'm talking about your husband, the one that you said doesn't understand what you go through. The one you said doesn't see you and puts on a front for others. You deserve more than what he's willing to offer. Because last night, if he had started chatting up the wrong woman, he would have been hooking up in the back alley or something. He tried it with me. And then he offered me a threesome with him and my 'girlfriend.'"

Tabby's jaw dropped. "*What?*"

"I lied and told him my girlfriend wouldn't appreciate it if I hooked up with him, and he said to bring her along."

Tabby laughed and shook her head. "He was clearly joking. Drew might be a jerk, and I know I expressed doubts about his faithfulness, but he's not a cheater. I would know if he was cheating on me." Her stomach churned. Even as she said it, Tabby had a hard time believing her own words.

"That's what you think," Jenni huffed. "I'm just telling you what I saw. He was going to have sex with me if I gave him the green light."

"Stop saying that!" Tabby said.

Jenni moved closer, trying to comfort Tabby with a soft touch on her shoulder, but Tabby jerked away. The way Jenni's eyes stared deeply into her soul sent chills up Tabby's spine. Jenni tried to touch her again, and this time she didn't pull away. Jenni drew her closer, until their bodies were mere inches apart. Jenni continued to close the distance between them until her lips pressed against Tabby's. Tabby's head spun as the kiss continued and she gave in to her desire of wanting to feel emotionally and physically connected with someone. At that moment, nothing else mattered except the feeling of Jenni's body so close to her own.

As Jenni's tongue slid across hers, Tabby realized what she was doing and pulled back. "Why did you...?" Tabby gasped, pushing Jenni away and turning.

"Tabby..." Jenni whispered. Tabby moved quickly to the door. She wanted to get out of there.

"Ugh!" Jenni groaned suddenly.

Tabby turned to find Jenni clutching her head and kneeling on the ground. No matter how much Tabby wanted to leave, she only had one option. Something was wrong with Jenni, and she needed her help.

CHAPTER FOURTEEN

Jenni

Jenni looked at Tabby as Tabby nervously bit on her fingernails. The kiss from moments ago was still racing through her mind, but she knew that Tabby had to be thinking about it even harder. Still, Tabby wouldn't look in her direction, and now they were stuck in a hospital room.

"I'm fine. It's just a migraine. Nothing I haven't been through before. There's no reason for me to be in this hospital bed."

Tabby shook her head. "You said that you've gotten them for years. You were brought down to your knees in pain. Wouldn't you feel better getting this checked out?"

"All the doctors have done what they could do. I've seen plenty."

"I would just feel better if we knew," Tabby murmured.

"Don't you have to get back to work?" Jenni asked.

"I'm on break. Now, just be quiet and wait for Dr. Wesley to get here." Tabby leaned back against the counter and dropped her eyes to the floor.

Jenni leaned back in bed and stared up at the ceiling. This wouldn't have happened if she hadn't felt the urge to immediately rush to Tabby and give her the news about Drew. What did she think that would accomplish? Did she think Tabby would fall into her arms and thank her for stalking him, then give her a passionate kiss? Well, the kiss had happened, but now things were abruptly changing between them.

A knock sounded on the door, and Jenni perked up. "Yes?" she called out.

Dr. Wesley opened the door and walked inside. "Hello, Jenni," he greeted. He looked over at Tabby, surprised. "Tabby? I didn't know you were in here."

"I was with her when she collapsed."

He nodded slowly. "I didn't collapse," Jenni blurted out.

From the corner of her eye, she saw Tabby roll her eyes, then focused her attention on Dr. Wesley as he spoke. "Well, let's hear what's going on. So, you have migraines? For how long?"

"Twenty years or so," Jenni said under her breath.

He looked up, arching an eyebrow. "And this is the first time you're having them checked out? Are they getting worse?"

"No, it's not her first time, but the doctors haven't been able to fix this, and the migraines are clearly getting worse," Tabby interrupted. "She was literally on her knees."

Jenni shifted her gaze to Tabby. Why was she suddenly so invested in how Jenni fared? She glanced back at Dr. Wesley.

"Tabby isn't wrong. The migraines have slowly been getting worse. I've taken ibuprofen, but it doesn't always do the trick. I've seen doctors, but they say there really isn't anything they can do for me." She shrugged. "So I just try to deal with them. Sometimes they're pretty debilitating, but I doubt anything will change, and I wouldn't be in this hospital bed if it weren't for Tabby here." She grimaced when Tabby shot her a look. "If you'd like to send me on my way, that's fine. I have a board meeting to get to."

"Well, before you rush off, I'd like to ask you a few more questions, if that's all right."

Jenni nodded, seething that she was there, and just wanting to bolt. "I'll answer whatever questions you have."

"When's the last time you saw a doctor?" he asked.

She shrugged. "For the migraines? Probably five years."

Dr. Wesley wrote that down, then looked up. "Right now, how's the pain? On a scale from one to ten."

"Fifteen? Maybe twenty," she teased.

He smirked. "I'll just write 'off the charts.'"

"Good idea," Jenni replied, glancing over to Tabby, who had gone back to chewing on her nails. The concern that Tabby appeared to have for her left Jenni on edge, with that one question hovering over her. Why?

"Have you taken any meds today for it?" he asked.

"No. I sometimes attempt to get through the pain without meds. I know it sounds silly, but it's how I try to manage."

Dr. Wesley looked at Tabby. "Will you go get her something from the cabinet?"

"Right away." Tabby hurried away and Jenni followed her with her eyes. Dr. Wesley cleared his throat as the door shut behind Tabby, drawing Jenni's eyes back to him.

"Tabby is a great nurse, but an even better friend."

"I can see that," Jenni responded.

Dr. Wesley eyed Jenni for a few moments. "Have you met Dr. Antonia Samson in the neurological department?" he asked.

"I don't think so," Jenni slowly replied.

"Well, she's fairly new to Capmed, but I have gotten to know her over the past two months, and she comes very highly recommended in the neurological field. She was telling me about this research study that she's part of. They are working on a new drug for migraines, and if you qualify, all costs are paid for by the research study. They're only taking a few candidates, and I could recommend you. It's fast-moving, though, so you would have to let me know right away."

The door opened and Tabby came back in with the pills and water. "Thanks," Jenni said, grabbing them from her. She quickly downed the pills, drinking a third of the water. "What kind of effects would I possibly see?" she asked Dr. Wesley.

He shrugged. "For that, you might want to confer with her. You know that all drugs have possible side effects. Sometimes you have to weigh the good with the bad."

"What's going on?" Tabby asked, looking between Dr. Wesley and Jenni.

Jenni saw Tabby's concern, but turned back to Dr. Wesley and said, "I would like to meet with her." She ignored Tabby's question because it wasn't her choice whether Jenni participated in the study, and she didn't want anyone to find a reason to convince her not to do the study. "Thank you."

"My pleasure. You'll hear from us no later than tomorrow. I'm sure she'll want to get you in right away. But in the meantime, I would suggest continuing self-medicating when you need it. You can't expect to feel well enough not to need the pills fully. They can be your crutch until you're able to have your appointment."

"Thanks again, Dr. Wesley."

He smiled. "Take care, Jenni. If you need anything, don't hesitate to reach out to me." He shook her hand, then looked over at Tabby.

Tabby's brows furrowed, which Jenni tried to ignore. Jenni swung her legs over the hospital bed and followed after Dr. Wesley. Tabby was only a couple of steps behind, but hurried up beside her, nearly bumping into her.

"What was that about?" Tabby asked. "Are you going to see another doctor?"

Jenni stopped walking and turned to her. "There's this specialist who Dr. Wesley thinks might be able to get me into a research study—a new drug or something for migraines. I'm having him set up an appointment."

Tabby frowned. "I don't know. I mean, if it's new, it's hard telling what the side effects could be, and I think it could be worse off for you."

Jenni sighed. "I understand your concern on the matter but it's my decision and my decision alone. If I think this could help me, then it might be worth it. I've been struggling with this for twenty years and I don't want to struggle for twenty more. Can you respect that?" Tabby nodded without hesitation. "Good."

Before Jenni could leave to get to her board meeting, Tabby spoke up. "I think we should talk about what happened before your migraine came on."

Jenni shrugged. "You were leaving the storage closet. That's how I recall it."

Tabby shook her head. "You know what I mean. What happened before that?" She fidgeted from one foot to the other and Jenni dropped her gaze.

"We don't have to talk about it. Emotions were running high. We can just acknowledge it happened and just leave it at that. I really have to get to my meeting."

"If that's how you feel," Tabby quietly replied.

It wasn't, but it was the easiest way she could get out of there without having to dive into the whole conversation again, especially hashing over the fact that Drew had flirted with her and that Tabby didn't want to believe it.

"It's for the best," Jenni replied. "I'll see you around."

She spun on her heel and hurried to the elevator. It *was* all for the best, even though, in that discouraging moment, her heart slowly broke into two. She had finally opened herself up to moving on from missing Wendy only to lose the one person who had pushed her there.

≫≫≫⫸ ⫷⫷⫷⫷⫷

By the time Jenni reached the conference room, most of the attendees were already there. She sat down in one of the few empty chairs. Less than a minute later, Brian walked into the room. He looked around and sat down at the end of the table and indicated the folders that were placed in front of each seat. Jenni opened hers to see a blueprint of the hospital's beginning plans. She looked it over and continued to the next page.

It was a single two-paged sheet—*Terminated Employees*, it read. She flipped it over to the other side, scanning the names that were on the list. Her eyes landed on Tabitha Brickly, and she froze. Hanna was listed too, as were several other people she had gotten to know over the years she had worked with the hospital. She looked up. Brian was speaking to one of the advisory board members. She cast another look over the list, her eyes shifting back to Tabby's name. This wasn't happening. She had to do something to change their minds. Tabby needed her job, and Jenni wasn't going to sit back and watch the hospital tear that away from her.

Brian cleared his throat, and all eyes went to him. "I have called you all here so we can go over the list of staff members that we'll be letting go first."

Jenni raised her hand, and he looked straight at her. "Yes?"

"Why these people? What's the reasoning behind it? I see several people listed on this list who are considered the best employees Capmed has. What's going on?"

Brian looked around the table until focusing his attention on her. "I'll be explaining much of this during the meeting. If you have any questions beyond that, you're free to speak with me after the meeting is adjourned. Okay?"

Jenni nodded and sat up straight in her chair, the headache still moving through her head. The pills would hopefully kick in soon, but then again, her stress was causing enough pain to keep the migraine going despite the medication.

Brian continued speaking, but only about finances and things that had already been discussed at prior meetings. Jenni kept her eyes down on her folder, itching to storm out of there, telling him that what they thought was the right way to go was, in fact, all wrong. Her throat grew dry halfway through his financial monologue. She did get up, but only to go over to the table and grab a glass of water. She went back to her seat and took a sip, letting the words flicker through her mind.

"Any questions on the financial aspect of this decision?" Brian asked the room.

Jenni looked up, relieved to see no one raising their hand. After all, they had already gone over countless times the finances that had led to this choice.

"Moving on," he said. "So, to answer some questions— why these employees? I can see disapproval on some faces over the termination list, and I want to start there. We feel that going with the ones who have worked here the longest will give us more financial gain. It is unfortunate that some of our best will be the ones hit, but that's just something we'll have to deal with. None of this is personal. In due time, I'm hoping that some of these employees will be able to be rehired. Of course, we won't know that until construction is nearly finished."

A hand went up, and Brian called out, "Yes, Charles?"

Jenni turned to face Charles, holding her breath.

"There are a few names on here that do cause me some concern. For starters, Tabitha." He hesitated, and Jenni released her breath. If anyone could get through to Brian, it was Charles.

Brian nodded in acknowledgment. "When we made these cuts, we didn't intend on cutting with our heart. We went solely by those who have years of service. That's all. Again, I fully believe that there will be a lot of unhappy doctors in the bunch. After all, they're losing strong nurses, but I know that we have trained all the nursing staff well, and they will be able to pick up where we're suffering from loss. Trust me on this. I've been doing this for almost thirty years, and I know what I'm doing. Let's move on."

Jenni's face, and her heart, fell. Brian was making these cuts without taking into consideration the lives it was going to hurt. She sat back, waiting for him to reach the end of his spiel, and hoping he would open up the floor for more questions. However, as the meeting died down, he didn't open the floor again.

"Folks, I have to get to another meeting. If you have further questions, you can filter them through my office. Have a great rest of your day, everyone."

Jenni jumped up and hurried over to him before he could leave. "I just have one question," she pleaded. He turned to look at her as everyone else filtered out of the room. "Do you think terminating the employees who have the most experience is good business? You're taking away staff that has built a connection with many patients. I don't see how that could be the right answer."

Brian sighed. "Jenni, I have always valued your opinion, but in this case, you have to stick to your own lane. This isn't your realm of business, and you need to leave the choices to the ones in charge. Our choices weren't made lightly. I know that while you and others might be frustrated, this decision isn't up for debate. Now, I need to go."

"How long before you start letting these people know they're out of a job?" she asked, wondering how long she had to change the current outcome.

He turned to face her. "Two weeks is when we're making the cuts." He didn't say anything more than that, just headed toward his office, while Jenni stared blankly at a couple of people who were still milling around the conference room.

She shook her head. That wasn't much time to work to change this unhappy fate. She knew one thing, though. There wasn't any way she could be around Tabby while this major secret was looming over her head. She also didn't want to be the one to spill the news to her. This would be something that would tear Tabby down even more. Jenni wasn't about to watch that, or even let it happen. If there was any way around it, she'd find it. But hiding it from Tabby was going to be tough.

CHAPTER FIFTEEN

Tabby

Tabby flipped to the nearest radio station, not caring about the music. She turned on her vacuum cleaner and ran it through the living room, unable to hear the music anyhow. The moment she started, her mind went to the kiss with Jenni two days earlier. Stop thinking about it, Tabby. It's not doing you any good. Yet, her heart and head had both replayed that memory over the past forty-eight hours.

Even though it laid heavy on her heart, she decided right away that she wasn't going to tell Drew about how Jenni had claimed he had flirted with her at the club. There were a couple of reasons why. One, she didn't want him angry that one of her friends had spied on him and to consider that maybe she was behind all of it. And two, there wasn't any proof that Jenni was telling the truth. She felt guilty for thinking Jenni would lie, though, and she wondered if she was simply in denial. The scenario she now weaved in her mind was that Jenni was secretly attracted to her and looking for a reason to come between her and Drew, but that was a crazy thought. Her marriage had already been on the rocks even before she had met Jenni.

She shifted her vacuum cleaner when she realized she had been running it over the same spot for the past fifteen minutes. She finished up in the living room and turned the vacuum off. Cleaning the house was something she found therapeutic, especially on her days off. She wasn't going to waste the day away by not doing any housework.

She grabbed the dust rag and ran it over the living room furniture. Soon, her thoughts went back to Jenni. Never had a kiss opened her up to so much excitement as it had when Jenni had kissed her. She had met Drew when she was a teenager, and he was the first—and only—guy she had ever kissed. It was overwhelming to think that her most erotic and delicious kiss came from Jenni.

Tabby stopped moving the rag mid-stroke and closed her eyes. The kiss came crashing back to her like it was the only thing keeping her alive. Jenni's tongue had stroked Tabby's in a way that had lit Tabby on fire. She shivered as her thoughts made her melt. She could practically feel the way her body would melt against Jenni's, and she had to snap her eyes open and catch her breath. If one kiss had Tabby feeling this way, what would a whole electrifying night do? You will never find out, Tabby thought firmly to herself.

She shook her head and moved to the hallway, dusting the table and light fixture that was in the foyer.

With every step she took, her thoughts leaned heavily toward the one woman she wanted to put out of her mind. Her phone rang from the living room, and Tabby was relieved to have something that could distract her from her memories of that moment in the closet. She rushed into the living room, turning the stereo off as she passed it. When she grabbed her phone, though, she spotted Britney's school's phone number. Her chest caved in.

"H…hello," she stammered.

"Is this Tabitha Brickly?" a man asked on the other end of the line.

"Yes, this is she."

"This is Adrian Parker, the principal at your daughter, Brittany's, school."

"Right, Principal Parker. How can I help you?" She attempted to make her voice sound stable and not torn up, but she couldn't think of any good reasons as to why Principal Parker would be calling.

"Your daughter was brought into my office. It appears she has gotten herself into a fight, and while I believe every story has two sides, we have a no-fighting policy. I would like to meet with you and your husband to discuss the matter."

Tabby nodded, her throat dry. She swallowed. "I will try to reach my husband, and we'll be right there. Thank you for calling. See you in a bit," she managed to get out.

Tabby hung up and sunk onto the couch. Brittany wasn't the type to get into altercations, and Tabby didn't want this to be the first of a string of disciplinary actions. As far as Brittany's school behavior went, she was always getting A's and was considered a stellar student. It bothered Tabby to think that maybe her daughter was headed on a rough path. The sooner they could change that, the better.

Drew's phone didn't ring, but went straight to voicemail. "Drew, it's me," Tabby said urgently. "Call me as soon as you get this. Brittany is in the principal's office, and we have to go speak with him. Please call me back ASAP."

When she disconnected the call, she wasted no time grabbing her keys and purse and hurrying out the door. Drew could meet up with her; she didn't have any time to lose. Brittany was in trouble, and Tabby was determined to get to the bottom of it.

❈❈❈❈❈❈ ❈❈❈❈❈❈

Brittany kept her eyes on the floor as Tabby looked in her direction. She had been there for fifteen minutes, and that was fifteen minutes too long. Drew still hadn't arrived, and she was anxious to get the meeting started. She checked her watch, then looked up at the principal.

"Let's get started. My husband must've gotten detained."

Where, though? She wasn't sure, but that wasn't what mattered, because she needed to focus her attention on her daughter.

"Are you sure?" the principal asked. "We can give him a few more minutes."

Tabby shook her head, and an unbidden thought came to her. If Jenni was somehow her spouse, *she* would be there. Tabby knew that in her heart. The more time she spent with Jenni, the more she saw how much Drew was failing as a father. If he wanted to fail *her*, then fine. But how could he fail their daughters?

Jenni would be there for a school meeting in a heartbeat. And Tabby had the feeling that marriage with her would be so much more fulfilling and wonderful.

Tabby clenched her fists. Drew hadn't once called her back. For all she knew, he was ignoring her pleas for him to come to the school. Either way, he wasn't there, and waiting a few more minutes wouldn't change that. "Let's begin," she said.

Principal Parker looked between Brittany and Tabby. "I'll make this short. I don't know what has gotten into Brittany, but this isn't like her. She was caught fighting during her lunch period and it took three teachers to break it up."

Tabby looked over at her daughter, who had a slightly smudged-looking bruise on her cheek. She looked back at Principal Parker, who continued. "As I mentioned, we have a no-fighting policy, and we make all children abide by that."

"Understood," Tabby replied. "I will ensure this never happens again. You have my word on that. And Brittany's. Isn't that right, Brittany?" Tabby gave her a stern look.

Brittany nodded, not looking up. She had been quiet the entire time, from Tabby's arrival to her conversation with the principal, and had barely made any eye contact.

Tabby looked back to Principal Parker. "I'm sorry for the trouble this has caused the school." She hesitated, then said, "May I ask who the other girl is?"

"Boy," he responded. "Richie Bates. I spoke to his parents an hour ago, and they have taken their son home."

Tabby's jaw dropped. "Brittany was fighting with a boy?"

She turned to stare at her daughter, who finally looked up. There were tears in her eyes. Tabby wouldn't embarrass her by asking her to explain herself right there, but there were so many questions running through her mind.

"Who started it?"

Principal Parker turned to Brittany, and there was a long silence that ensued before he glanced back at Tabby. "Neither one was in the right, and because of it, both are facing suspension for one week." Tabby nodded, dazed. Suspension? This wasn't her daughter. She could have pictured Callie in a situation like this, but not Brittany.

The principal continued. "The teachers have put together her homework assignments for the next seven school days. If there are any questions regarding the assignments, she can email the teachers directly."

"All right. Thank you." Tabby took the papers that he offered her. "And again, please accept our apologies." Tabby nudged Brittany, who looked up and gazed at her principal.

"I'm sorry," Brittany said. "I didn't mean to cause any harm."

"Kids will be kids," Principal Parker stated. "But it's our job to ensure this doesn't happen again. You are better than this, Brittany. Remember that."

She nodded, then dropped her gaze again. Tabby stood up and shook his hand. "Thank you, Principal Parker."

"I'm sorry we had to meet under such circumstances, but thank you for coming in as quickly as you did. We look forward to you coming back to school, Brittany."

"Thank you, Principal Parker," she mumbled.

Tabby and Brittany left the office, and Brittany walked a

few steps ahead of Tabby. Tabby stayed quiet until they reached the car. Once inside, though, she turned to her daughter.

"We are going to talk about this," Tabby said firmly.

Brittany rolled her eyes and looked out the window. Tabby reached out and touched her arm, but Brittany slowly pulled away. Brittany moved her hand to her eye, and it hurt Tabby when she saw her flicking away a couple of tears. Tabby turned and looked out the front of the window. She drove home, the silence as strong as ever as they moved through the streets of Chicago.

When she pulled into the driveway, she thought maybe Brittany would bolt out of the car, but to her surprise, her daughter walked slowly to the house, staying in step with Tabby. Once they were in the foyer, Brittany turned to her.

"Are you and Dad getting a divorce?" Brittany asked.

"What?" Tabby asked. "You are thirteen and you do not need to be worrying about things like this."

Brittany shook her head. "I'm thirteen and no longer a child, Mom. I deserve to know. I need to prepare myself, and I've heard you fighting. I've seen when you go to the spare room to sleep. My anxiety is going through the roof, Mom, and I need some answers. Otherwise…" Her words trailed off, and she looked away. Tabby spotted a few more tears. Tabby reached her hand up to her daughter's cheek and stroked it softly.

"Is that what the fight was about?" Tabby asked.

Brittany turned to look at her. "It was stupid. I was already having a rough day and was walking through the halls, practically in a daze. I got to the lunchroom and Richie came busting through. He bumped into me. What's stupid is I know it was an accident. He wasn't trying to knock me down or anything. But because my thoughts were all over the place and I was so angry, I pushed him. That seemed to startle him. He didn't deserve to get in trouble, too. He never hit me. I tripped and fell, causing this bruise." She touched her cheek. You should have seen him. He just was trying to defend himself —really."

She covered her eyes. "I should have talked to you before it got to be this bad."

Tabby pulled Brittany into her arms and hugged her tightly. "I'm sorry that you felt you had no choice but to push someone. Fighting is never the answer, but you *should* have talked to me. I would have been there to hear whatever you wanted to talk about."

When Brittany pulled back, more tears stained her cheeks. "I don't want you to think that you have to stay in this marriage because of us," Brittany whispered. "If you're not happy, then we have to be strong for you."

Tabby pulled Brittany back in her arms again and Tabby felt her own tears stinging the backs of her eyes. "We'll get through this together."

Brittany nodded. "Just be honest with me, Mom, please," Brittany pleaded, pulling back and looking up at Tabby. "Do you think about divorce?"

Tabby stared into her daughter's eyes, and her heart ached. She bit down on her lip, then nodded. "But I want you to know that we're not doing anything yet. And this isn't your battle. But I will be honest with you now. You can trust that."

"I love you, Mom," Brittany sniffed.

"I love you, too. Now, go up to your room and start on your homework because you have enough to last you awhile. Are you hungry?" Brittany nodded. "I'll bring you up a sandwich."

"Thanks, Mom." Brittany threw her arms around Tabby's waist, then went up the stairs. Tabby watched her go, waiting for the door to shut before she looked away. It was hurting her children, this dance between Drew and her. That was the one thing she didn't want to happen. But now, she was going to have to take a stand. Drew couldn't even be bothered to come to the meeting, which spoke volumes. There wasn't anything more important than making sure her children were taken care of. That was where Tabby's heart was, above all.

CHAPTER SIXTEEN

Jenni

J enni stared at the names of the employees, as she had done for the past week. She was no closer to figuring out what she was going to do about making sure that Tabby didn't lose her job, along with others. Maybe she could somehow move everyone on the list to other hospital areas that needed help. But then the hospital would still be keeping the same amount of payroll, which would put it back at square one—needing to make staff cuts.

She leaned back in her kitchen chair and considered all the options, but nothing new came up. From only cutting half the staff to shifting the employees into other positions, every option she considered brought on a hundred reasons why it wouldn't work. Even making a pro and cons list wasn't working. She knew the cons far outweighed the pros in this situation. There was nothing positive, in her eyes, about these employees losing their jobs, no matter the money Capmed would save.

It isn't your problem to fix, Jenni. Yet she felt otherwise, because if she had more money to put into the hospital, then perhaps she could save these jobs. She scooted her chair back up to the table and looked the list over, thinking hard. If there was more money going into the hospital....That would truly solve so many things. But how? Where could that money come from?

It was true that Jenni didn't think she was the only one in the Chicago metro area who had money to filter into the hospital. Others were just as wealthy as her, if not more. If she could get more money coming in, the hospital wouldn't have to worry about the money going out.

Jenni sat up. It was an idea, and one that might work.

Jenni grabbed the list and folded it up, then slipped it into her pocket. She was doing this for all the nursing and administrative staff that were on the list. And if it didn't work, it was their jobs on the line. However, if it did, the hospital could have its renovations *and* keep its valued staff.

Jenni got in her car and headed to Capmed, ideas streaming through her mind. They could start with a benefit fundraiser, maybe even have a concert or two that would draw in money and donations. When she reached the hospital, she actually felt hopeful. This could actually work. Right now, it was the only idea out there that she couldn't see reasons for being shot down.

The first stop she made was the cardiology floor. If she got the doctors on board, then maybe they would be able to help her push her ideas with Brian and the rest of the board.

Charles's door was open when she reached his office. She knocked, and he looked up and smiled.

"This is a pleasant surprise," he said.

"Well, I wanted to see your thoughts on an idea I have." He sat straight in his chair and tilted his head. "We want the nurses to keep their jobs, right?"

He nodded. "Can't disagree with that," he said. "But I have worked with Brian for years, and I know that he isn't one to give up easily once he makes up his mind. I don't really know what we can do about it. I guess writing up recommendations for the nurses might be the best bet. I know I'll do what I can to ensure that Tabitha gets a job shortly after getting her pink slip."

"What if there doesn't need to be any pink slips, though?"

Charles looked at her endearingly. "I'm not surprised you're going to try to change the outcome. You've always been one to do what's right. What do you have?"

Jenni started telling him the ideas she had about a benefit and fundraiser. He listened intently without interrupting. He nodded a few times and kept his attention focused on her, absorbing everything she was saying. When she was finished, he, too, looked hopeful.

"I don't hate the idea. It could actually work. It's just—getting Brian convinced. We could probably get free entertainment. Maybe even Tabby's husband would perform."

Jenni nodded, but deep down, she knew that would likely not happen. She didn't want Drew to be a part of it, and by now, she hoped that Tabby would agree.

"Are you going to take it to Brian?" Charles asked

"I am, but I want to have some support behind the

proposal before I do. That way it's not just some frivolous idea that someone came up with."

"There's nothing frivolous about it. I like the idea. If you need me to put my statement out there, just let me know."

"Thank you."

There was a knock on the door, and Charles looked up. "Come in," he called out.

The door opened and Tabby entered. She immediately looked over to Jenni, and Jenni quickly stood up. The intensity of her stare was as real as if Tabby had lasered her gaze on her.

"Sorry to interrupt," Tabby said, turning from her. "Mr. Carlson is complaining of chest pain radiating up and down his left arm."

"I'll be right there," Charles said.

She nodded and then looked over to Jenni. Jenni nodded slightly, but without acknowledging it, Tabby turned and hurried out of the room. Charles stood up and chuckled as he moved toward the door.

"If I didn't know Tabby was married, I would say that there's some tension between you. Sexual tension—just so I'm being clear."

Jenni moved quickly to the door. "What? You're absolutely misreading things," she lied.

He shrugged. "Well, as I said, I know better. Anyway, let me know if you talk to Brian, and what he says."

"I will."

Charles headed for his patient's room, and Jenni looked around the halls of the floor, but Tabby was nowhere to be found. She shrugged it off and continued toward the elevator.

As she pushed the button, her phone started to ring. She took it out of her handbag but didn't recognize the number.

"Hello?"

"Hello, is this Jennifer Jennison?"

"Yes? May I help you?"

"This is Bridgette from Dr. Antonia Samson's office." Jenni had been anticipating that call but had given up hope after the third day of waiting. "I am calling because I have you down on the list to be a part of the research study Dr. Samson is currently working on. She would like to get you in for an evaluation this afternoon. Are you free?"

"Um, yeah, I suppose so."

"Two o'clock?" Bridgette asked.

Jenni checked her watch. That was only an hour away. She was already at the hospital, so that part worked out, but deep down she worried that she would find the meeting to be a waste of her time and that she wouldn't be eligible for the study. But worrying would only give her reason to stress out even more. Stress brought on the migraines, so she needed to steer clear of that.

"I'll be there," she said.

"Great." Bridgette told her where Dr. Samson's office was located, then finished with, "We'll see you then." She hung up before Jenni could rethink her concerns. She had one more stop to make, and then she would focus on her appointment.

She took the elevator down to see Brian, hopeful that she was on her way to saving all of the jobs that were in jeopardy. She reached Brian's office and waved at his secretary, who sat at her desk.

"Hello, Jenni," she said.

"Hey, Phoebe. Is Brian free? I just have something really quick to run over with him. Won't take any more than two minutes."

"Yeah, he's free. Go on ahead."

Jenni smiled, heading for Brian's office. She knocked on the door and heard him mumble something, which she took as a "come in."

He looked up, his face falling at the sight of her. He shook his head. "Are you here to tell me how I'm doing my job all wrong? We've been through this, Jenni. There isn't any other way."

"But I think there is," Jenni pressed on.

He sat up and clutched his hands together. "Okay, I'm listening."

"I have donated a lot of money to Capmed. I think that if other people had the option, they would gladly pool their money into the hospital, too. I think you should hold a benefit concert and fundraiser. Get donations. It will help with the renovations, and you won't be forced to fire half your senior staff. It will work, Brian. I know it will."

He sighed. "And who's going to pay for this concert and fundraiser?"

"I will gladly offer some of my money to assist, and I think we can do it relatively inexpensively. People can volunteer, including the hospital staff. I've already talked to some of the doctors, and they think it's a great idea."

Brian raised his eyebrows. It was a lie, but not entirely. She was confident other doctors would jump on board if they knew they could do something to not lose their staff. "I know that you think it will be a waste of time, but I'm asking you to at least try."

He shook his head. "I don't know. It might be too little to do any real good for us."

"But we can try. That's all I'm saying," she urged.

After a moment, Brian sighed. "I'm not saying yes. I'm saying that I will consider it."

Jenni smiled. That was better than hearing a no. If he was willing to think about it, she could continue working on him to make sure he eventually agreed. There wasn't any reason not to give it a try. She was already eagerly planning everything out in her mind.

Jenni wrung her hands on her lap as she waited for the nurse to come back into the room. Two hours had passed, and she was nervously anticipating the results of her lab work. But she knew she would have to wait another day or two to receive that.

A knock sounded on the door, and she looked up. "Come on in."

Novalee came into the room. Her name was another that was on the list that Jenni had spent hours looking over. It was difficult to interact with all these people when Jenni secretly knew that their lives could be uprooted later.

"Here are the brochures that Dr. Samson wanted me to pass along to you. They go over the clinical trials, adverse reactions, expectations, frequently asked questions, et cetera. Once your lab work comes back, providing everything is within the levels that we need them to be, we'll call you and schedule your appointment for the next visit. Do you have any questions for me?"

Jenni shook her head, her hands shaking as she took the papers from the nurse. "Thank you." She looked down at the first brochure, on which there was a photo of two women who had bright smiles. That seemed uplifting, but it also meant they advertised well.

"You're free to go. Expect to hear from us in a couple of days. If you have any questions, the direct number is located on the back cover of each brochure. Have a great rest of your day."

"You too."

Jenni left the room feeling even more hopeful than she had when she had gone in. At least she was being considered as a valid candidate. And if she were accepted into the study, it could make her life better in the long run. Nothing could be wrong with that. Even if she experienced side effects, she was ensured that they were minimal, and only five percent of participants experienced those. Even the brochures stated the same. Why look for something wrong in something that was probably totally fine?

Jenni reached the lobby of the main floor and headed straight for the exit. Her thoughts were so focused on the fundraiser and research study that she didn't pay attention to the person on her left, heading in the same direction, until they collided with one another. She dropped her brochures and reached out to grab them at the same time that Tabby reached down.

"Sorry about that," Tabby said. "Wasn't paying attention."

"That makes two of us," Jenni replied, looking tentatively at Tabby.

Tabby looked down at the brochure in her hand, then quickly looked up. "You got into the clinical trial?"

"Working on it. I just finished the first appointment and had lab work done. We'll see how that goes." She took the brochure from Tabby's hand.

"I'm happy for you," Tabby replied. "I hope it all works out."

"Thank you," Jenni said warmly.

They walked outside the hospital together, heading toward the parking lot. "How've you been?" Tabby asked. "Have the migraines been staying away?"

"Pretty much," Jenni answered. "With any luck, they'll even be better going forward."

"Yes. It's good to stay positive about that," Tabby replied.

The conversation died as they stepped into the parking lot. "How've you been?" Jenni asked. As they reached an aisle in the lot, Tabby stopped and motioned to her vehicle.

"I've been doing all right," she said.

Jenni saw Tabby's eyes darken, but she wasn't in a position to ask about that, though she wanted to. She wanted to share conversations together, even though the kiss lingered in her mind.

"That's good," she finally said. She could ignore her desire to inquire further as long as Tabby didn't burst into tears in front of her. If she wanted to talk to Jenni, surely she knew that was an option.

"It was good catching up with you," Tabby said. No matter that the conversation had barely lasted a few minutes.

Jenni nodded and forced a smile. "Anytime you want to talk, you have my number." Tabby's mouth opened, and she quickly closed it and looked away, which disquieted Jenni. "All right then, you take care."

Before Tabby could utter a response, Jenni quickly walked away from her. Gaining distance was ideal at that moment. If she had to say one more minute, she would pull Tabby into her arms and plead with her to be honest and to tell her everything that had been going on with her over the past week.

As she walked away, Tabby grew farther and farther behind her, as did the idea of asking her those questions. No, it was better for her to let Tabby come to her if she so chose. Then Jenni would allow Tabby all the freedoms she needed to tell her everything. That's when Tabby would fully be able to share everything, and Jenni would be able to wrap her up in her arms and tell her that she was there for her. She would always be there for her.

CHAPTER SEVENTEEN

Tabby

Tabby leaned in and hugged Callie. "Goodnight, sweetheart."

"Goodnight, Mom!" Tabby squeezed her arms around her and closed her eyes as she held her younger daughter. "See you in the morning."

"Not if I see you first," Callie said, a big smile on her lips.

Tabby was glad to see that Callie was not yet phased by her marriage problems. Tabby would only hope for Callie to stay young and innocent like that forever. She blew her a kiss from the door, then left her room.

Tabby had been glad her shift had ended early, so she could have dinner with the family and possibly have a heartfelt conversation with Drew. One problem had popped up, though. Drew had never come home for dinner. He must've assumed Tabby would make it home to take care of the kids, or maybe he was at the point where he didn't care about being a good father, which troubled Tabby.

Drew? Just wondering where you were. I thought you'd be home for supper. We really need to talk. It was the message she had left on his voicemail only an hour earlier when she had attempted to get through to him. The call hadn't even rung— just went straight to voicemail. It had been a common occurrence over the past week. She now wondered why she even bothered trying to talk with him when she knew he would disappoint her yet again.

Tabby knocked on Brittany's door. "It's open!" Brittany hollered.

She entered and looked around the spotless bedroom. Though Brittany had been suspended over the past week, she hadn't allowed herself to neglect her chores. If anything, she had made sure to keep up with the cleaning. Tabby was grateful for that.

Britney was a good girl and mature for her years. Tabby knew she could trust her older daughter to stay home alone when Drew wasn't there. And lately, that was often. She kept the neighbors on standby but allowed Brittany to stay home alone. Brittany hadn't let her down.

"Doing homework?" Tabby asked.

Brittany nodded and held up a book. "I have a book report due next month. Mr. Notting said that we should make sure to read the book twice through. I was just starting up the second read. She dropped the book and met Tabby's gaze.

"I'm so proud of you," Tabby said, sitting down on the edge of Tabby's bed.

Brittany scrunched up her nose. "Even though I caused a fight?"

Tabby nodded. "I know that you've been through a lot, and it's not right to punish you for things that even we adults don't understand. You will do the right things when you get back to school next week." Tabby leaned in and brushed a kiss against Brittany's forehead. When she pulled back, Brittany frowned.

"Dad missed dinner tonight."

"Well, yeah, but he's busy. He has another show tomorrow night and just wanted to rehearse with the band. That's all."

Brittany's answering smile didn't quite reach her eyes. "Love you, Mom."

"Love you, too." She squeezed her daughter's hand and got up from the bed. As she headed to the door, she cringed. She didn't like lying to either one of her daughters, but this was a time she knew that being honest would do more harm than good. She stopped and looked over her shoulder. "Let me know if you need anything before going to bed."

"I will. Night, Mom."

"Goodnight, sweetheart." Tabby spent a few more seconds just staring at her daughter before turning away and leaving the room. Once she returned to her bedroom, she looked over to her dresser. Two pictures sat on top, one of her and Drew's wedding day and the other of the family. She picked up that picture and stared at it. Her fingers ran over each of her daughter's faces, and it broke her heart that she had been put in this position of wondering. What if? What if one day the picture of four was minus one?

What if she really did divorce Drew? She wanted her girls

to grow up in a stable home with lots of love, but raising them alone would be hard. Would Jenni stick around? She loved children, and there was a spark between them neither of them had fully addressed.

Tabby smiled to herself, letting her mind wander. She imagined waking up every day to Jenni's beautiful smile. They would be true partners and best friends, and she could see the four of them spending time as a family, going to events together and having fun. Jenni would never bail on her when times got tough. Tabby was confident of that.

Her smile faded, and she came back to reality. After the kiss, Jenni seemed to be fine with letting it go and moving on. She might not feel as strongly as Tabby did, and they weren't even in a relationship. How could Tabby be fantasizing about Jenni becoming her wife? It was a silly thought.

She put the picture down and pulled out her phone. Still no missed call from Drew. She pulled up his contact info and called him. It went to voicemail right away.

"Hey, Drew. Me again. Now I'm just worried. Where are you? I'm starting to think the worst. That you've gotten into a car wreck or something. Please give me a call. Perhaps you forgot to tell me you had plans, and if that's the case, so be it. But I'm going crazy here. *Call me.*"

She disconnected the call and looked over to the empty bed. She felt a tear break free from her eye and slowly trail down her cheek. She closed her eyes and brushed the tear away. He was fine, just ignoring her call. But the agony inside of her was pulling her into a deep, dark hole. Which would be worse? That Drew was ignoring her calls, or that something bad had actually happened? At least the latter wouldn't be intentional. That thought tugged at her heart. To wish for something like that was killing her inside, but where was he? And why wasn't he calling her back?

The moment the light flicked on in the bedroom, Tabby opened her eyes. She turned to watch Drew as he sauntered over to the bed. She had to scoot out of the way so he didn't fall onto her. "Hey, baby," he said, kissing the air in her direction.

"That's all you have to say?" Tabby asked. "I've tried calling you not once or twice, but three times. You had me scared to death. And you're drunk? Are you kidding me?"

She got off the bed and stood up, staring at him, until he slowly started to laugh. "What's crawled in your panties?" he asked.

Tabby walked over and shut the door, attempting to keep her children from hearing. She turned back to him. "Where were you?"

"Out," he said. "Some of the guys wanted to grab some drinks. That's all." He shrugged.

Tabby shook her head. "I'm not buying it. I called you at seven o'clock. It went straight to voicemail. I called you again at eight-thirty. Again, voicemail. Then I called you at one. So don't go giving me that. If you were out having drinks, you could have had the decency to at least call back. Give me a straight answer, Drew. I mean it. Where were you?"

He arched an eyebrow. "I was out," he said.

"Okay. With a woman? You reek of alcohol and women's

perfume, so don't you dare try to lie to me. Are you cheating on me? Is that it?"

He pulled himself up and sat on the edge of the bed, his eyes downward, at the floor, all while Tabby stared at him from behind. His lack of response was enough for her to know that she was on to something. It was also clear that Jenni wasn't making anything up. Her husband was a flirt and now a cheat.

"I have my answer," she said. She stormed over to the closet, opening the door and pulling a bag out.

"Where are you going?" Drew asked. Before she could turn to him, he had come up behind her. Tabby smelt the fragrances even more strongly than before. It caught her breath, and she turned away from him.

"Anywhere but here. The kids are sound asleep, so I'll let them be, but I can't stay here with you."

"Baby, just listen," he pleaded, touching her shoulder. Tabby tensed up, her arm tightening from his touch. "It isn't what you're thinking. It's not like I'm having an affair." Tabby looked over her shoulder and his eyes softened. "I promise you." He brushed his hand against her cheek, and she tightened up again. "It's not an affair."

"That's what you keep saying. What is it then?" She turned to face him. "Be honest, Drew. I can't handle this, and you know what? Neither can your children. Brittany is already asking if we're going to get a divorce. What's going on?"

He dropped his gaze from her and turned to head back to the bed. He collapsed on it, and covered his eyes. Tabby watched his body shaking and didn't move to console him. She simply watched in agony, waiting for him to speak or do something. He sniffled and then sobbed.

"It happened once," he wailed. He looked up, tears streaking his cheeks. "I was weak and should have been stronger. I didn't mean for it to happen, but you and I have grown distant, and you haven't exactly been willing to give me what a man needs. I slipped. I shouldn't have and I'm sorry, but I'm not entirely to blame."

Tabby turned to her dresser drawers, tears already stinging her eyes. There, she had it. He had been unfaithful to her, but was what he said the whole story? She wasn't sure she bought it. She shook her head and started grabbing random items from her drawer, enough to keep her supplied for a couple of days.

"Where are you going?" he demanded again. She hesitated and turned to look at him.

"I told you. I'm going anywhere but here. You slept with another woman. I'm not going to let you walk all over me like that. I will call tomorrow to talk to the kids." With that, she hurried out of the room and to the bathroom, where she grabbed a few toiletries, and then was down the stairs and out the door. She reached her car, and that's when the floodgates opened and she couldn't hold back her tears. She looked up at the house and saw how dark it suddenly seemed. Drew hadn't come running after her, and she wasn't about to rush back inside and listen to more excuses.

She backed out of the driveway, headed in an unknown direction. The farther she drove from the house, the more confused she was. The only person she knew she could possibly stay with was Hanna, but that would mean she would have to get real and tell her everything about her failing marriage.

Thirty minutes later, though, she pulled up in front of Hanna's house. The house was completely dark, and there was only one vehicle in the driveway. It didn't look promising that she'd be able to get a hold of Hanna, but she had to try anyway.

She knocked on the door and waited. When no one opened the door, she knocked again. It was two o'clock in the morning. *She's probably* asleep, you idiot. But Tabby had pounded hard on the door, loud enough to have awoken the dead. She was certain of that. She headed back to her car and sat in the driveway for a moment. Hanna and her husband could have gone out and used Hanna's vehicle, leaving his at the house. But it was highly unlikely they would be away from the house that late. They were in their mid-forties, after all. Tabby couldn't fathom them being out at this time.

She backed out of the driveway and began driving aimlessly, not knowing where she was going to wind up. The few hotels she passed had No vacancy signs out. Tabby turned into a parking lot and sat there, the darkness overwhelming her. If she waited much longer, she'd be sitting with the sunrise.

Tabby grabbed her phone and pulled up Jenni's number, her movements slow and hesitant. She didn't want to wake her up, but Jenni had said to call if she needed to talk. This seemed as good a time as any to give her a call. It's the dead of night. Think again, Tabby. Still, she pressed the Call button.

Jenni answered after three rings. "Hello?" Her voice was hoarse, and it was clear she had been sound asleep.

"I know it's late," Tabby said in a rush, "and I probably

just woke you up. For that, I'm deeply sorry. But I need someone to talk to."

"Tabby? Where are you?"

Tabby broke down into tears, the weight of everything she had been holding slowly crumbling down on her, and her heart shattered. Drew didn't deserve her tears. On the other hand, her children were the ones who would pay the price, and Tabby feared that things were going to come crashing down all over them.

CHAPTER EIGHTEEN

Jenni

Jenni handed Tabby a hot cup of coffee, and Tabby looked up. "Thank you."

"You're welcome." Jenni took a sip of her own and sat down across from her. She had been surprised to get a call from Tabby, but she hadn't hesitated in directing her to her house. She had heard the tears in her voice and had just wanted to help her out. Now, all she could do was watch her and be there to lend a listening ear.

Tabby sighed as she took a drink. "Sometimes I wonder what I did to deserve the way Drew feels he can treat me. But I never wanted to believe that he was capable of cheating on me." She huffed. "I don't know why I found that so ridiculous. After all, he wanted to force me to have sex with him the other day. Of course he would be capable of this."

Jenni just listened, waiting for Tabby to share whatever she wanted to share. Tabby shook her head. "I should have believed you when you tried telling me that he was flirting with you and wanted to hook up."

"Tabby, I don't find it odd that you didn't want to believe that. He's your husband. You want to believe the best in him. I understand. And I'm sorry that you had to deal with this tonight."

Tabby took another sip and stared down at her cup. Jenni watched her appear almost childlike.

"I'm the one who's sorry," Tabby said. Jenni, looked up, surprised. "I came to the house so late tonight. I just abused your friendship."

"Tabby, don't be silly. You were out driving around in the middle of the night, and you needed to be somewhere safe and warm. I'm just happy I could accommodate. You can stay as long as you need."

Tabby smiled and held up the coffee. "Just one night should suffice." She sniffled, then added, "Maybe two."

Jenni smiled. She would allow her to stay there until she was ready to leave. She was sure Tabby would need to get home to her children, but Jenni wouldn't turn her away.

"And thanks for the coffee. I really needed it." Tabby took another sip, and Jenni nodded.

Jenni leaned back in her chair and let the quiet seep into her kitchen. Tabby hadn't even changed out of her pajamas. It was clear she had rushed out of there in a hurry. Jenni didn't blame her. When Tabby had spilled the news to Jenni, her voice had broken, just as Jenni believed Tabby's heart had broken at that moment. Even though they didn't have a picture-perfect marriage, it was still a marriage. And with children involved, it was bound to be a rougher road.

"I look like an absolute mess," Tabby mumbled.

"You're not a mess," Jenni protested. Don't say that."

Tabby lifted her gaze, along with the corners of her lips. "Let's talk about something else," Tabby replied. "Have you heard anything about the clinical trial?"

"Actually, I just got a call this afternoon. I'm supposed to go to an appointment on Monday, which is when we'll get started."

"That's good news." Tabby's eyes lit up. For the first time, she didn't look like she was thinking about the husband she had left back at the house. "I'm hopeful it can really work."

"Me too." While that was good news, Jenni still believed that Tabby, along with many others, were on the verge of losing their jobs. A board meeting was set up for the following Wednesday, and she hoped that she would be able to convince everyone to move forward with her ideas for saving the jobs. She'd be pretty surprised if the stress from that didn't give her a migraine.

She looked to Tabby, who was back to surveying her coffee. There were so many ways she had considered telling Tabby about the expansion project that could eliminate her job, but she always changed her mind. What Tabby didn't know wouldn't hurt her. And Tabby had so much on her mind already. She didn't need one more thing to worry about. Hiding this information was her way of protecting Tabby. Keep telling yourself that. It doesn't make it true.

"I'm mentally and physically exhausted," Tabby murmured.

"You should try to get some rest. I'll show you where the guestroom is."

"You're right," Tabby replied. They left the two mugs on the kitchen table and headed down a hallway to a room, where Jenni had already put Tabby's single bag.

"The restroom is right down the hallway on the right. My bedroom is upstairs—the first room on the left—if you need anything. And there are extra blankets in the cabinet right there." She turned back to Tabby. "Can you think of anything else?"

Tabby shook her head. "Thank you."

"Have a good night," Jenni said. As she turned, Tabby reached out and touched her arm, startling Jenni.

"Jenni?" Tabby began.

Jenni looked at her, and her heart hitched, right along with her breath. Seeing the affection on Tabby's face made Jenni want to melt. She tilted her head.

"I can't thank you enough for this. I really appreciate it."

"You don't need to thank me," Jenni said, her tone going up a notch as she concentrated on the heat that came from Tabby's touch. "I'm happy to do it."

"I could never repay you, though. But I can do this." She moved close, kissing Jenni and sending a wave of shock coursing through her as Tabby snaked her hand up Jenni's shirt.

Jenni wanted to go further. It was every fantasy that she had imagined being played out, but she breathlessly pushed Tabby away.

"We can't," she argued. "Not like this."

Tabby looked away. "Great. Now you're going to reject me."

"Tabby," Jenni pleaded. "I'm not rejecting you. I would give anything for us to go on kissing and ultimately wind up in bed together. I am *very* attracted to you. You have to know that. When I kissed you the other day, it wasn't by accident. You have to believe that."

"They why stop?" Tabby asked.

Jenni let out a breath. Her dreams were laid out right in front of her, but doing the right thing wasn't always the easy thing to do. "Why? Because if we do this, you're no better than Drew, and you and I both know that you *are* better than him. Talk to him. If you dissolve your marriage, then that's a different story. But I'm not rejecting you. I'm stopping us before you can regret any decision you make tonight."

"I know—you're right," Tabby whispered.

Jenni backed out of the spare room. "I'll see you in the morning, and we'll talk." She turned away and headed upstairs. The farther she got away from Tabby, the better. Otherwise, she would succumb to her needs and forget everything she had just very reasonably explained to Tabby. But she needed that release and didn't know how much longer she could wait for it.

⋙⋙⋙ ⋘⋘⋘

Jenni took her time in the bath the next morning. She hadn't been able to get much sleep last night because every time she closed her eyes, her thoughts went to Tabby. Or, more importantly, Tabby under the bedsheets in the spare room. The images wouldn't leave her mind. With a twenty-minute bath behind her, she was prepared to go downstairs and see Tabby. At least, she was mentally prepared. She wasn't so sure about her heart and desires, which craved the woman she had so abruptly turned away.

When she went downstairs, her one hope was that Tabby would still be sound asleep. No such luck, as she entered the kitchen and spotted her at the stove. Jenni cleared her throat and waited for Tabby to turn around and look at her.

"Good morning," Jenni said cheerily.

Tabby smiled at Jenni, something she hadn't been able to do the night before when they were chatting. "Morning. Give me three minutes and breakfast will be served." She turned back to the stove.

"You didn't need to do that. I could have whipped us up something."

Tabby laughed and shook her head. "I'm used to it. As a mother and wife, cooking comes second nature." She continued working on their breakfast as Jenni took her seat at the kitchen table.

"Did you sleep all right?" Jenni asked, trying to make small talk.

"Well, I'd be lying if I said I slept like a baby. Maybe a newborn baby that wakes up every fifteen minutes crying." Her words seemed upbeat, but Jenni could only imagine the pain that was laced through them.

"I'm sorry," Jenni said.

Tabby shrugged. "It's nothing you should be apologizing for. I'm the one who called you in the middle of the night, needing a place to stay. I'm the one who should be apologizing to you. For many reasons, in fact." She looked over her shoulder and met Jenni's gaze. "I'm sorry for the abrupt kiss that I pushed on you last night. That wasn't called for, and you were right. I wouldn't have been any better than Drew."

Jenni sighed. "Don't apologize for that. Like I said, if I weren't working hard to be strong, I definitely would have kept it going."

Tabby smiled. "It was just bad timing. Ain't that the truth."

She turned around and busied herself, filling two plates with eggs, sausage, bacon, and hash browns. Jenni was mesmerized as Tabby grabbed things from cupboards like she had been in Jenni's kitchen her whole life. Tabby put a plate down in front of Jenni and looked at her.

"Orange juice? Milk? Or coffee?" she asked.

"Whatever you're having," Jenni said. Tabby turned and grabbed two glasses, then filled them both with orange juice.

Jenni scrunched her forehead as Tabby pushed her glass toward her. "I have to ask," Jenni started. "How do you know your way around this kitchen so well?"

"Well, as I said, when you're waking up every fifteen minutes, you can get a lot accomplished. That includes touring the kitchen to learn where everything is so I would know when I made breakfast this morning. Eat up before it gets cold."

Jenni looked down at her food. It was more than she was used to eating every morning, since she would typically reach for cereal or oatmeal. "Looks delicious," Jenni said, digging into the eggs. She nodded, wiping her mouth. "This was unexpected, but very good. Thank you."

"It was the least I could do," Tabby said.

The conversation died down as they both ate silently.

Fifteen minutes in, as Jenni chewed on a strip of bacon, Tabby spoke. "I called the girls this morning."

"Oh yeah? How'd they take the fact that you left in the middle of the night?"

"Well, turns out Drew didn't tell them that. He just said that I had to go into work this morning." Jenni opened her mouth, and Tabby nodded. "Yeah, I was surprised, too. Then again, if he had told them the truth, that I ran off in the middle of the night, he would have had to mention how he had a part in it. I'm guessing he doesn't want the girls to know that he's sleeping around. Not so surprising."

"Yeah, I suppose so," Jenni replied, finishing off her bacon.

"He has a show tonight and I'll need to watch the girls, so I'll head on home so I can be with them. I'll probably leave here about six or so."

"Whatever you want," Jenni softly whispered. She stared down at her breakfast and felt Tabby's eyes on her. She looked up, and sure enough, their gazes met.

"Do you think I'm foolish?"

"I don't think you're foolish, Tabby. You have to be home for your girls. That's only common sense. I just hope you don't let Drew walk all over you. You deserve much better than that, so promise me that you'll speak to him only when you know what you're going to say."

Tabby let out a breath. "I'm not sure I'll ever fully know what to say to him, but I can tell you this." She hesitated, staring down at her plate of food while Jenni waited for her to respond. Tabby's eyes darkened in those few minutes that she struggled to find the words. When Jenni saw a tear slip down her cheek, she got up and went over to wrap her arm around Tabby's shoulder. "My marriage is over," Tabby said, her voice breaking.

Those four words were spoken as if a weight had been lifted off her shoulders. Tabby spoke them again, then covered her eyes and started to sob. Jenni never left her side, keeping her arm tightly wrapped around her. It was going to be all right. Jenni would do anything to make sure Tabby believed that.

CHAPTER NINETEEN

Tabby

T abby sat on the couch, just staring at the fireplace, the logs burning slowly, the light flickering and lighting up the living room with a soft glow. She wiped away a few tears that had been falling periodically, as memories of her marriage kept trailing through her mind. When the front door slammed shut fifteen minutes past midnight, she jerked to attention and turned to watch Drew walk around the corner.

"Hey," he said.

"Hi." Tabby sat up straighter and kept her eyes fixated on his. "How was your show?"

"Good. Long." He sat down in the chair across from her. "It's dark in here." He stood and went to one of the lamps, turning it on. "That's better." He resumed his seat and looked her way, but she quickly looked away from him. Her eyes were red, and her cheeks were splotchy. "Or not," he muttered.

She shrugged. "It is what it is." She was relieved to see he wasn't drunk, stumbling around the living room with slurred speech and blurred vision. It might help them have a decent conversation, one she had practiced numerous times through the night. "What we have going on here isn't a marriage. It hasn't been a marriage for a long time. And if you're willing to be honest, you'll admit that you know this."

"Babe," he started. Tabby tilted her head and locked eyes with his. "Tabby. We can get things back to where they were."

Tabby sighed and fell back against the couch. There were so many times she would have given anything to hear him say those words, but now she was just tired, and she didn't have any fight left inside of her. What she felt with Jenni was so much more than what remained between her and Drew. They could try to fix their marriage, but Tabby didn't believe Drew would really commit to change. And her heart was already with someone else. Someone who would treat her with the kindness and respect she deserved, making each day more magical and fulfilling than the last.

"You want counseling? Then fine. We'll do it."

"We've been there, done that. Don't you see? We've been constantly jumping through hoops, trying to save our marriage, and I'm tired, Drew. I'm tired of not knowing when we'll fight next or if we'll get through the turmoil. It's not working, and I don't know that I want to fight for it anymore."

"So, what are you saying? You want a divorce?"

Divorce was too final of a word. "I think the kids are going to need an adjustment period. We'll start with a separation.

Then once the kids are settled in and understand what's going on, we'll move toward divorce."

Tabby dropped her eyes. Just saying the word left her drained. In her parents' relationship, divorce was a dirty word. Tabby believed she would always do anything to make her marriage work. But it wasn't just up to her, and if Drew wasn't always going to give a thousand percent, then why should she be the only one?

"What are the next steps then?"

"I think it only makes sense that the kids and I stay in the house and you go to a hotel. It will be easier to transition the kids if they don't have to leave the only home they know. Agreed?"

"Makes sense," he mumbled. "Guess we'll start that tonight then." He stood up from his chair.

"It's after midnight, Drew. You'll have to pack, so you might as well stay here tonight. Tomorrow, we can let the kids know what's going on."

When Drew glanced at Tabby, his eyes seemed to be looking right through her. It startled her as she stood up from the couch.

"It's best to just get it over with. I'll leave and go to a hotel and then come here tomorrow to get some clothes. Why delay the inevitable?"

"I don't hate you, Drew. We just grew away from each other. You're the father of my children, and I'll always love you. You don't have to make this awkward between us."

He shook his head. "You're kicking me to the curb, Tab. It is what is. That's what you say, right? No need to second-guess your thoughts."

Tabby frowned. That wasn't what she was doing. She wasn't second-guessing herself. She knew she was following her heart and doing what was right.

"I'm not kicking you to the curb, Drew."

"Yes, you are," he snapped.

Tabby looked away from him, fearful that she would start crying and show him the emotions she had been feeling all night.

"I make one mistake. I sleep with one woman and you're like 'off with your head.' Makes me wonder if there's more to it."

"Drew! It's not about sleeping with one woman. It's about the whole marriage. It's about finding that we're growing away from one another, instead of further in love. I'm sorry if you don't understand that, but I'm not trying to be unreasonable."

"Fine! If that's what you think." He turned away from her, and she slowly followed him to the door. She was going to watch him drive away and that was going to be it. At least, that was the way it was looking.

"Drew," she whispered.

He turned back to her, and before she could step back, he wrapped his arms around her and hugged her. "I'm sorry."

Tabby keenly felt those words as he slowly began to weep. Maybe she was all wrong. Maybe he was a changed man and counseling would help them through it.

Instead of telling him this, she held onto him and said, "Thank you for your apology." He slowly pulled back from the embrace. "I don't hate you," she reiterated.

He nodded, turning away and walking out the door. In that moment of silence as she watched him get in the car and then drive away, Jenni's words echoed in her mind. Don't let Drew walk all over you. Would changing her mind and trying counseling again be something that would give Drew his way? No matter what, she had to take a stand, and letting him drive away was the only thing to do.

The cafeteria was busy with patients' families milling about and staff on their lunch break as Tabby took a sip of her coffee. She glanced down at her watch and sighed. Her lunch was going by way too quickly. She only had ten minutes before she had to get back to work, but she would soak up every last drop of those ten minutes. She took another sip and then put down her cup and closed her eyes. Just four more hours of work. Then she could leave and get the girls from school. Surely the afternoon would fly by.

"Is this seat vacant?" She opened her eyes and looked up as Jenni approached the table.

"Oh. Sure." Tabby sat up and waited for Jenni to take a seat. It'd been nearly a week since Tabby had spent the night at Jenni's, and it had been the longest week of her life. "How are you doing?" she asked.

"Good. It's been a few days since I started the treatment for the migraines."

"Oh, that's right. You were starting that Monday, right? How'd it go? Experienced any side effects yet?"

She shrugged. "I've been a tad tired, but overall, I'm doing well. They said that it can take a few weeks before I finally see it working toward migraines, but I feel that so far, so good. I haven't had a migraine this week, so that's good."

Tabby nodded. "Happy to hear that." She looked down at her empty tray and then at her watch. Time was ticking by, and she only had six minutes left of her break—not nearly enough time for everything Tabby needed to say to Jenni.

Tabby finally took a breath and looked up. "I want to apologize. I did mean to call you and let you know what was going on. I've just been so emotionally drained and physically tired. So, I'm sorry. I want to talk about us. I just need a little time to wrap my head around everything."

Emotionally draining was an understatement. She couldn't get the memory of telling her girls about the divorce out of her mind.

"Your father and I are separating," Tabby had said earlier that week as Drew and she sat across from the girls Sunday morning. To her surprise, Brittany had stayed strong for Callie, wrapping her arms around her sister and waiting for Callie to start crying. But the tears never came. Callie was stronger than Tabby knew.

"Will we see Dad?" she had asked.

Together, both Drew and Tabby had assured them that they would get equal time together, which both Callie and Brittany seemed glad to hear.

That had been such a hard conversation, but it was out of the way now.

Tabby stood from the cafeteria table, checking her watch. "My lunch is over," she told Jenni, "but just know that everything is going to be okay. Drew is staying at a hotel and the kids know that we're separating. From there, I guess we'll just take it one step at a time. I appreciate your willingness to give me a shoulder to lean on. It means everything to me."

"Anytime, Tabby. You know where to find me." Her genuine smile was something that made Tabby feel even warmer inside.

"I have to go. I'm so happy your migraines are getting better." She touched Jenni's shoulder. "Please give me a little time and be patient." She waved and then hurried from the table, dropping her tray into the trash can.

Tabby went back to the cardiology floor and went straight to the desk, looking through the files of her next patient. It was the job that would help her take care of the kids, just as it always did. She would do her part in making sure neither Callie nor Brittany ever looked at their father negatively, but she was going to be the strong woman she needed to be. It wasn't going to be easy, but she could do it.

CHAPTER TWENTY

Jenni

Jenni leaned forward and looked at the plans in front of her. It would be hard work, but if done correctly, the board wouldn't have to do any of it. She would be more than happy to pick up their slack, and with the staff's help, it would surely be a fundraiser that no one would forget.

She took a sip of her water, then flipped through the pages of various donors that had already come in. She was pleased with the funds she had secured so far. With the way things stood, she wouldn't have been surprised if that was all they needed to ensure that all nurses and administrative staff would remain employed.

Her phone rang and she looked at the caller ID, surprised to see Tabby's name flashing on the screen. She was giving her time and space, but it was difficult to be apart.

"Hello?"

"Hey, Jenni. I was just thinking about you." The hairs stood on the back of Jenni's neck. "I mean, not thinking about you, but thinking about everything. You know, all that's been happening and stuff."

"Oh. Sure." Jenni released a breath. Her heart started racing and she had to calm herself down. Clearly, her mind was in a different space than Tabby's. "How are you doing?"

"Okay, I guess. Just sent the kids off to be with their dad tonight and was sitting here thinking about, well, you know."

Jenni didn't know. She was already confused, and the conversation was only getting stranger by the second. She didn't respond, hoping Tabby would see that she was making no sense.

"I'd like to talk, if you have time. Are you available to come over tonight?"

"Oh. Uh, yeah, I'm not really doing anything." She glanced over to the pile of work that Tabby couldn't know anything about. "I'll head over now."

"I'll see you in a bit." Tabby disconnected the call and Jenni got up from the table and looked down at her worn-out T-shirt and faded jeans. That wasn't going to cut it. She hurried up the stairs to her bedroom, where she rifled through her clothes. She tried on not one or two, not even three, but four different variations of outfits. Then she finally settled on a loose sweatshirt and jeans. It didn't look like she was trying too hard. It would look like she had grabbed the first thing she saw in her closet and thrown it on.

Satisfied, she left her room, steeling her resolve. She couldn't go into Tabby's home thinking that anything would happen between them. She had to be strong. Until the marriage was dissolved, nothing could happen.

With Tabby's text, her purse, and her car keys in hand, Jenni was out the door ten minutes later. She put Tabby's address into her GPS and drove twenty minutes to Tabby's home. She pulled into the driveway, noticing the porch light was on. Tabby's house looked cozy from the outside, and Jenni wasn't nervous walking up the trail that led to the front door. When she knocked, it didn't take long for Tabby to answer the door.

Jenni's eyes couldn't do anything but wander down Tabby's front. She wore a tank top and tight jeans. It was far from the scrubs she was used to seeing Tabby wear, and it made Jenni groan internally. Her breasts were tight against her tank top, and Jenni instantly wondered how those breasts would taste. She had to bite back those thoughts and remind herself she wasn't going there.

"Would you care for a drink? Wine? Water? Wine?" Tabby laughed. "Whatever you want. I think Drew even has a few beers, if that's more your style."

"I appreciate the offer, but the drugs they have me on don't let me have alcohol. Not that that needs to stop you or anything. By all means, if you want to drink, go ahead. I'll just have some water."

"Water for two, then. I wouldn't drink in front of you. Don't be silly." Tabby motioned toward another room that was connected to the foyer. "Have a seat and I'll be right there."

Jenni walked into the living room and looked around. The fireplace was already lit. On the mantle was a string of pictures. Her eyes went to the family portrait. They looked happy. Brittany looked to be ten years old, so the photo must have been taken a few years ago, but the whole family appeared to be smiling.

"Here you go," Tabby said, interrupting her thoughts. Jenni grabbed the water from her. "You saw the picture, huh?"

"You all look so happy," Jenni pointed out.

Tabby took a sip of her water and looked at the picture. "I would say we were happy, to an extent." She smiled. "It's hard to know what to do with the pictures, though. I keep them up for now because the kids are living here. But eventually..." Her words trailed off, and she shrugged. "They'll have to come down or go into the girls' rooms."

Jenni quirked up an eyebrow. "So, you're thinking this is really over?"

"Most likely, yes. We've already had a long talk with the girls and they were surprisingly accepting of the situation."

Jenni sipped her water, processing those words. Though she had feelings for Tabby, she ultimately wanted Tabby to do what she thought was best. If that meant trying to work things out, she would have to accept that. That was the power of change. People could change their minds at any given moment, and Jenni didn't want to get her hopes up on just a possibility.

"You know," Jenni began, "marriage is always hard work. There's little that can be disputed with that. If it's worth fighting for, then by all means, you should fight for it. If you wake up every morning thinking about your husband and the love you have for him, then you should surely keep that love intact."

Tabby's eyes shifted toward the fire. Jenni wished she could read her mind. What was she thinking? Did her words resonate with Tabby at all?

"What if you start to feel that maybe love doesn't have to be a part of your marital union? You have two kids that you share. You can equally love them but live in the same house and just find ways to cohabitate together," said Tabby.

"So, you're saying you would be all right if Drew went out and lived his life, and you lived yours, but you stayed together just for the children?" Tabby looked down, and Jenni waited for her response, but it never came. "Tabby, that isn't any way to live. I'd like to believe you're smart enough to realize that."

Tabby looked up, shooting a glare in Jenni's direction. "What else is there to do if we did stay together? It feels like it's over, but Drew keeps making these comments to suggest we have other options other than divorce. And my parents always taught me to do everything I can to fight for marriage."

"At the expense of your happiness?" Jenni argued. "Why should you put your happiness on the back burner, just because you want to save a marriage? Do you love him still? Can you honestly look at me and tell me that you are in love with your husband?"

Tabby tilted her head and slowly shook her head. "I care for him and probably always will, but to say I'm in love with him…" She shook her head harder. "It's tough to utter those words."

Jenni saw the agony in Tabby's eyes. She didn't want to make Tabby feel worse about her situation. She had come here because Tabby needed someone to talk to, a shoulder to cry on, a heart-to-heart, and that was what Jenni had to give her.

"I know I don't talk much about Wendy," Jenni began.

"But she was destined to be the one I would grow old with. We were so similar that it was sometimes hard to imagine we were two different people and walked through two different paths. Wendy immediately had my heart from the moment that we met. A chance encounter that never should have happened suddenly turned my life around. I saw that I had meaning in my life once again. Never in my wildest thoughts would I have ever dreamt that she would disappear from my life so suddenly. One minute she's here and the next she's gone, and I think about her every day. It wasn't until I bumped into a certain nurse that I believed I could ever move on."

Tabby's cheeks turned bright pink as Jenni continued.

"There you were. When I saw you, I didn't know if you were gay, straight, or bi. I just knew that you were the first person who made me feel something inside. And when I got to know you, I started to feel these emotions that I thought had died right along with Wendy. It saddened me to learn you were married, but as I grew to know you and saw the way you were being mistreated in your marriage, all that mattered was showing you the love and kindness that you deserve out of life."

"Wow," Tabby said breathlessly.

"I'm not trying to tell you all this thinking that it will change the outcome. I think you truly need to do what you think you need to when it comes to Drew and how you want things to work between you two. For me, I think you need to respect yourself when you make your decision. But you're the one who needs to make it."

Jenni stood up from her seat, and Tabby quickly followed suit. "Where are you going?"

"I don't think I can stay here. The temptation is too much, being around you."

She started to move toward the foyer, when Tabby reached out and grabbed her hand, startling Jenni. "Don't go. Please. I know what I need, and I need you. I know you said to wait until everything is finalized, but....You may think it's foolish, but I *do* need you."

Jenni's heart slowly rattled in her chest as she studied Tabby. Foolish or not, with Tabby showing Jenni her desires, Jenni couldn't turn from it. She didn't want to. She moved in closer, following the lines of Tabby's fingers and clutching her hand in hers. She breathlessly kissed Tabby, her moan echoing through the living room, her tongue slowly wrapping around Tabby's. She pulled back, giving Tabby time to rethink what she had said. When Tabby only gazed back fiercely at her, Jenni grabbed her face between her palms and pulled her closer, kissing her harder.

With one push, she had Tabby seated on the couch, and she straddled her legs around the woman of her desires. Their tongues quickly collided, and she slowly snaked a hand up Tabby's tank top, breaking from the kiss only to toss the tank off to the side. They didn't know where the night would lead them, but Jenni knew she was looking forward to exploring every curve that would get her there.

⤞⤞⤞⤞⤞ ⤝⤝⤝⤝⤝

With one arm wrapped around Tabby, Jenni pulled her closer and kissed her hard, her tongue smoothly sliding along Tabby's. They had moved their sexual endeavors to Tabby's bedroom, something that felt so intimate and so right. There were moments when Jenni thought she should stop and see if they wanted to continue in the spare room, but Tabby seemed to be completely engrossed in it. If Tabby wasn't pulling back, then Jenni wouldn't either.

Jenni pulled herself up and shifted her body on top of Tabby. She broke from the kiss to gaze at Tabby and saw that her eyes were sparkling. Jenni ran her hands over Tabby's bare breasts, and she moved in and pressed her lips between Tabby's cleavage.

Tabby giggled, then shifted her body beneath Jenni. "You have no idea how much I needed this," she whimpered. Jenni shifted both palms and slowly started to knead Tabby's breasts between her hands, leaning forward to kiss Tabby with a passion that was finally realized.

"Me too," Jenni whispered, moving her tongue in to claim another moan from Tabby. She had lost count of how many times Tabby had moaned. It was something that sent electric shivers up and down Jenni's spine.

"You're breathtaking," Jenni whispered, slipping her tongue in and out of Tabby's mouth, filling with heat at the sound of Tabby's groans, which lit her insides on fire. Her body was tight and petite, to be expected with the age gap that trailed between them, but Jenni didn't allow age to be a factor in their electrifying night together. It just felt like everything had finally come together, and knowing that Tabby was starting to realize her worth made Jenni even more invested in being with her.

Tabby broke from the kiss. "This has given me so much to think about. It's opened my eyes to the world in so many ways.

And I feel like I'm ready to have some breathing room to figure out what I'm going to do."

"Which is what, exactly?" Jenni asked.

"Well, for one, sit down and talk to Drew. Before he left, he said he was actually open to doing some marriage counseling, and if he truly is, then maybe I need to get some insight into that."

Jenni's jaw dropped at this turn of events, and she rolled off Tabby and stood. "You're telling me this while we're having sex?"

Tabby stood too, tears in her eyes. "I'm sorry for being this way. I'm just scared, and I don't know what to do. Everything is so confusing. Do I owe it to my family to cover all of my options? I needed this tonight, but I also need to take into consideration what's best for everyone. I can't be selfish."

Jenni nodded. "You're right. You have your children to consider, and apparently, you have Drew to consider. But I don't like feeling used. When you kiss me, you need to be one hundred percent certain that it's me you want. My emotions are involved in this, too." She turned and stormed out of the room, anger slowly turning into disappointment. When she reached the living room and started to get dressed, she heard Tabby's footsteps.

"Don't rush off like this," Tabby pleaded.

By now, Jenni's eyes were clouded with tears. "I don't know that we have anything to talk about. At least not yet. Clearly, tonight meant more to me than it meant to you."

"That's not true," Tabby started, reaching out and touching Jenni's arm. "It meant the world to me, but I have to be realistic here. Should I just throw away a marriage that's lasted nearly thirteen years?"

"When that man has been sleeping with probably every single woman in town, then I would say you don't owe anything to him."

"He said it was just one woman," Tabby argued.

Jenni covered her eyes and shook her head. "Tabby, I've been around the block a few times. Surely you can't be that naïve." Tabby looked down, abashed. "But until you figure all that out, there's nothing I can do here. The call is up to you."

With that, she turned and walked away, leaving the house. She hesitated once she reached her car, thinking that if she went back now, she could pull Tabby into her arms and plead with her to choose her. But it wasn't going to play out like that. This was one decision she couldn't make for Tabby, no matter how much it was breaking her heart.

CHAPTER TWENTY-ONE

Tabby

Seeing how upset Jenni had been when she left the house had made Tabby pause. She had never had a night with someone who made her body so aflame, and it was exhilarating to think about the two of them continuing where they'd left off. Yet she owed it to herself and her kids to fully understand where her marriage was going. If divorce was the outcome, then having this transition period was necessary.

Three days had passed since that night, and Tabby had been able to avoid Jenni and her own erotic thoughts because, for some reason, she hadn't seen her at the hospital at all. At least that was a relief, as it gave her some breathing room to think about her marriage.

On that third day, she entered the breakroom and caught a group of employees all gathered at one table. They were looking over a paper and whispering to one another. Tabby went over to the vending machine and was browsing the selections when she heard one of the women gasp. She turned around and looked toward the table. "What's so exciting?" she asked.

It was Greta, who worked down in the pharmacy, who was the first one to speak. "Have you heard about the renovations that will be starting at the end of this week?"

Tabby shrugged. "I've heard a little about it. I haven't been paying much attention when it comes to what's been going on around here. Why?"

Myra, who worked in ICU, looked over at Tabby. "Well, a list has been leaked." She looked around the table. "We don't want to get anyone in trouble, so we're just going say someone showed it to someone, who then showed it to someone else, who then showed it to someone else." She shrugged. "You get the picture. Anyway, this list shows that some hospital staff are on the brink of losing their jobs."

Tabby's eyes widened. "Who's on it?"

Myra grimaced. "I'm on it, as are Hanna and Greta." She shook her head. "Looks like they're getting rid of the people who have the most seniority."

Tabby frowned. "Give me that." She skimmed through the first page, then moved on to the next page. There her name was. Shocked, Tabby said, "Wow. Guess it doesn't pay to work your butt off anymore." She put the paper down. "Whose brilliant idea was this?"

Greta replied, "No idea. But it looks like the board members have all signed off on it." She turned it over to the last page and held it up. Tabby looked over the names, and right at the bottom of the list was Jenni's signature. She grabbed the list back and stared at the name, shaking her head. It wasn't possible. She had spent enough time with Jenni that if this were going on, Jenni would have told her. Did the intimacy between them account for nothing? "This was signed two weeks ago," Tabby muttered.

"Yep," Myra said.

"Guess I should be glad that I'm a newbie," a man said, slumping down in his chair. "But that means I'll be losing all my friends that I've made."

"Wait a minute," Tabby started. "We're not going to go down without a fight, right?"

"Tabby," Greta began. "We're not even supposed to be seeing this list."

"Well, we *have* seen this list. And I don't know about you, but I'm going to talk to someone about it. We can't just sit back and wait for them to give us our termination. That's not happening—no way, no how." She shook her head vehemently, but everyone else looked concerned. "If I have to fight this myself, then I will, but where's the Capmed fight that you all used to once have?"

Some staff stammered some excuses, and Tabby turned from the group, the list still in her hand. "Where are you going?" Greta asked.

When Tabby turned back to face them, Greta had gotten up from the table, looking serious. Greta continued, "I got this list secretly and I would prefer to make sure no one is aware who this came from. So you have to let me know where you're going."

Tabby tossed the list back to the table and Greta quickly

snatched it up, clutching it to her chest like it was the last thing giving her life. "I will keep you out of it, I swear. But I have a family that needs me to support them, and I can't just wait for Capmed to give me my walking papers. I have to at least try to get some answers. If I do it alone, then so be it."

She turned and headed out of the breakroom, the door swinging behind her. She reached the elevator and entered, pushing the button for the main floor. She looked up as the doors were about to close and saw the rest of the group headed her way, including the three people who weren't at risk of losing their jobs.

"If you're doing it, then we're all doing it. We're in this together," Myra said softly. "We've got your back."

Together, they reached the main floor and walked down the hallway that led to Brian's office. Tabby led the way, and they approached his assistant's desk. The assistant's eyes widened when she saw the group. "May I help you?" she asked.

Tabby looked at the assistant's name tag. "Hello, Phoebe. We're here to see Brian," she stated firmly. "And we're not leaving until he sees us, so you might want to let him know that."

The woman's eyes narrowed in on the group and she nodded as she dialed Brian's office. She turned her back, so they could only hear the muffled sounds of her voice. "They said," she started, her voice raising an octave—to the point where Tabby nearly caught word of what she was telling Brian —but then lowering to a whisper. "I'll let them know," she finished.

She swiveled her chair around to look at them. Tabby

braced herself, convinced she would have to do some complaining if Phoebe attempted to turn them away. "You can head down the hallway. He'll see you." Tabby turned and looked at the rest of the staff, who were right at her heels. They all nodded with eagerness and resolve.

"Thank you," Tabby replied. They turned and headed toward Brian's office. Tabby had a million things she wanted to say to Brian, most of which started and ended with, How could you treat us like that?

"Come in," Brian called as she initiated the knock on his door. When they walked inside, he looked up, his eyes glancing over each one of them. He scooted back from his computer and locked eyes with Tabby. "I hear you wanted to see me."

Tabby looked over her left shoulder, then her right. No one spoke up, so it was all up to her. She turned back around and nodded. "Brian, we like to believe you think we work hard at our jobs. The ones who stand before you strive to make sure we do what is asked, before it's asked. We kick butt."

She bit her lip and shifted her stance from one foot to the other. "But it's come to our attention that the hospital that we all put in the work to help thrive is looking to let many of the senior staff go. And we're here to demand answers."

He arched an eyebrow. "I assume you've seen a list or something."

"Something like that. And we know that all of the board is behind this. What we don't understand is, why? Are our blood, sweat, and tears not enough?"

For emphasis, she leaned forward and pounded on his desk with her fists. His eyes went down to her fists, and he looked up, raising his eyebrows sternly. Tabby slowly pulled back. "Sorry. We just demand some answers."

Brian cleared his throat, then looked at the staff standing before him. Tabby waited for him to look at her again. "If memory serves me, not all of you are on the list." He looked over at the guy who stood directly behind Tabby, on her right. "Brett, you've been here how long?"

"A year, sir," he said.

Brian nodded. "That's right. You're not on this list. What sort of reasoning do you have to be here?"

"I'm standing up for the ones being terminated. I have made friends here and I can't picture this hospital without them."

"I've learned in my position that it doesn't pay to make friends." Brian's eyes landed back on Tabby. "With that being said, the list isn't finalized. And it shouldn't have been leaked."

"Are you saying we're all not getting terminated?" Tabby asked.

"I'm saying that we haven't made the final cuts. We're still working on it. We still have some things to iron out. Rest assured that once we make those cuts, we'll better understand where we are. Understood?"

Tabby frowned. It wasn't quite the resolution she was looking for, but she nodded. "We all are pleased with the jobs we do here. You shouldn't let finances rule over everything."

He responded with a frown of his own. "I'll consider that. Now, if you'll please leave; I have some work I need to get done."

With nothing resolved, the group left his office. Before they parted, they all agreed to keep silent about the list so that other staff wouldn't be alarmed. In a place like Capmed though, Tabby fully expected the entire hospital to know about the cuts by the end of the day.

Tabby reached the elevator to go to the cardiology floor just as her phone rang. She glanced at the caller ID and saw Jenni's name flashing on the screen. She had probably gotten word that the list had leaked and was working to do damage control. Tabby wasn't going to allow her to beg for Tabby's forgiveness.

Tabby stepped off the elevator with a voicemail message. She considered automatically deleting it, but ultimately settled on listening to what Jenni had to say about the staff cuts. She was surprised that Jenni didn't bring up the cuts at all.

"Hey, Tabby, it's me. I was hoping we could catch up later. There are some things I need to discuss with you that have been weighing on my mind. Give me a call. I look forward to hearing from you."

Her tone was so sweet and clean, which confused Tabby as she slipped her phone into her pocket. It was only a ploy to get what she wanted, and Tabby wasn't falling for it, even if Jenni was the one person Tabby wanted to talk to. She was possibly losing her job, and Jenni was the only one who could console her and tell her why, but Tabby wasn't going to reach out—not if it meant falling for Jenni's ploy.

CHAPTER TWENTY-TWO

Jenni

Brian stood at the front of the conference room as Jenni looked over her notes. She had everything written down, ready to plead her case, and anticipated that everyone would willingly agree with all of her points. She needed to make sure she didn't leave any stone left unturned.

"Thank you all for meeting here at the hotel," Brian started. "They've started construction at the hospital, and I just thought this way, we wouldn't be in their way when they're working on the boardroom. I've spoken to Lesa Niel, who owns this hotel, and she's agreed that we can have access to their conference room going forward. There's a lot to go over, so let's not wait a single minute. I know that Jenni has a lot to discuss, so I want to give the floor to her. Jenni…"

Jenni stood up, dipping her head in acknowledgment. "Thank you, Brian."

She looked around the table at the rest of the people who were present, including the doctors, who would state their cases. "Thank you all for being here. So, I have been working on getting donors who are more than willing to provide financial assistance to Capmed." She held up the list and rifled through the pages she already had. "I know that it's only a start, but I'm prepared to fight every step of the way. Saving these jobs is what I'm passionate about."

She dropped the list to the table. "I have given this a lot of thought. I've spoken to D.M.J. Country Club, and they are willing to offer a place for us to have a fundraiser and charity drive."

A hand shot up, and she pointed to Charles. "Yes?"

"What type of things were you thinking for the fundraiser?" he asked. "Food? Auctions? You said charity drive? What does that all include?"

"Glad you asked, Charles. There would be a dinner. I have one of the donors listed here, who is willing to cater the fundraiser. For the auctions, I was thinking we could involve the whole city. We can have items donated to charities. It will get all of Chicago involved, and what's even better is if the staff knew that their jobs were in jeopardy, they would probably be willing to help out in any way they could. This will be something that will require little work for everyone, as I'll be putting in a lot, if not most, of the work. But this is what I love to do."

Jenni scanned the room and saw several board members nodding their agreement on the matter. "There's some work to do to iron out all the details, but I think we're nearly there. If you're all on board, then I will go full force and get this started."

She stopped her gaze on Brian, unable to read his facial expression. After a moment, he simply nodded. "You have put a lot of work into this matter; I can see that."

"I'm passionate about this because I've been in a position in which I was going to be terminated and no one was there to help. I want to be their voice."

"You should have been in my office yesterday, then," Brian snickered.

"I'm not following," Jenni said.

"A group of employees stopped by my office yesterday. Turns out the list of potential terminations was leaked, and the staff wasn't going down without fighting first."

Jenni considered those words. *Who were the pages leaked to?* She tried to push that thought from her mind and from her conscience. "I see," she finally answered. "Well, I would have been their voice, no doubt." She turned her gaze to the rest of the staff. "So, is everyone on board?"

"Let's take a vote," Brian said. "All those in favor, raise your hand." Slowly, everyone's hand went up, including Brian's.

Jenni beamed and nodded, relieved that they had gotten somewhere and eager to put things in motion. "Great! Now, we just need to come up with a date."

They worked on finalizing those details, and as the meeting came to a close, Jenni realized that she had singlehandedly made things work out. None of the doctors had to voice their concerns, and it was something that brought her a sense of pride. The meeting didn't go over an hour, and when they adjourned for the night, Jenni thought about the logistics of several ideas she wanted to carry out.

As she left the room, she spotted Charles coming over to her. "Well done, indeed."

She shrugged. "It was nothing."

"I wouldn't say that. This was all you. Kudos. You should be very proud."

She nodded, just satisfied that it had worked out in her favor. "But I wonder who leaked the list," Jenni pointed out. "And I wonder who saw it."

She mostly wondered if Tabby had gotten her eyes on it. If she had, she wanted to get to her and make sure she knew that the danger of Tabby losing her job had subsided. She had tried calling her the previous day to meet with her and tell her about the whole fiasco. But Tabby had never called back. She was worried that Tabby thought she was out of a job.

"You're looking at him," Charles replied, chuckling.

Jenni's jaw dropped. "You? But why? Didn't you think that would cause an uproar within the nursing staff?"

"That's exactly why I did it. I wanted to give them the fury to want to fight for themselves. It wasn't fair that they were being left in the dark, and I wanted to light a fire under them. It looks like it worked."

Jenni bit the corner of her lip. It did, but without any repercussions? She wasn't so sure.

"Gotta run. Cecilia almost has dinner ready. Talk to you later." He waved and then hurried away from her.

Jenni slowly walked toward the lobby, thinking about what Charles had said. Here she had done everything to keep the news from Tabby, but Charles had made sure the whole hospital would know. Now what? If Tabby had seen it already, would Jenni be able to convince her that she had kept the list from her to protect her?

As she reached the door, she dug into her pocket for her phone, then groaned. She had left it in the conference room. She turned to cross the lobby again and abruptly ran into a man. He hesitated and looked at her, tilting his head as if he recognized her. Jenni quickly looked away. He may not have recognized her, but she recognized him right away. "Excuse me," she mumbled.

"No problem, dear," he said. He winked at her and then proceeded toward the front desk, where a blonde stood. When he approached her, he kissed her with a slow and passionate hunger—making Jenni's jaw drop—then proceeded to the elevator.

Jenni attempted to shake that image from her brain. Drew and a blonde were headed up to a room, certainly to do the obvious, in Jenni's mind. She shivered as the nasty thoughts plagued her mind. While Tabby was taking care of his children, he was still off having sex with other women. For once, Jenni didn't care about the outcome. She wasn't going to sit back and let what Tabby didn't know hurt her even more.

<hr />

Jenni stepped up to Tabby's front door. She paused, just staring at it. She was busting in to disrupt Tabby's life yet again when Tabby could still be having dinner with her kids. She hesitated, then turned to leave.

The image of Drew and the blonde popped back into her mind. They had been making out as the elevator doors were closing. The woman looked to be no older than eighteen. Tabby deserved to know her husband was out there still treating her so disrespectfully. She turned back to the door and knocked.

A few moments later, the door flew open. It wasn't Tabby, but Callie. "I know you," Callie said.

Jenni smiled. "Callie, right?"

Callie nodded, then called out, "Mom? Your friend's here."

It didn't take long for Tabby to round the corner. "Hey, Tabby," Jenni said in greeting.

"Callie, run on upstairs and shower. I'll be up in a bit to tuck you in."

Callie turned to Jenni. "Bye!"

Jenni waved back as Callie went up the stairs, and Tabby turned to her.

"What are you doing here?" Tabby asked. "You should go."

Jenni cowered a little as Tabby tried to push past her to get to the door. "Why? There are some things you need to know. This won't take long."

Tabby huffed. "There's nothing you can say to me that will surprise me. I saw the list, Jenni. What I don't know is why you didn't feel the need to tell me."

"I was trying…" Jenni started, but Tabby held up her hand and cut her off.

"I don't need to know. You signed off on it, which meant

you were all for it. Well, that's nice to know. You don't care whose job is at stake. Brava, Jenni. You clearly fooled me."

Jenni frowned. "I wasn't for it. I didn't sign off on anything."

"Oh really? You're going to lie to me?" Tabby stormed past her and went into the living room. A short time later, she returned with a paper and pointed to the bottom of it. "That's your signature, right?"

Jenni took it from her and stared down at her signature. She looked up and nodded. "That's my signature, but I didn't sign this."

"So someone forged it. Bet Brian would love to hear you say that." Tabby shook her head, and the disappointment on her face made Jenni's heart ache.

"I'm not saying someone forged it. I'm saying that they took my signature from another form and transposed it onto the paper."

"That sounds like a lot of work, don't you think?" Tabby asked.

"Yeah, but it's the truth," Jenni said.

Tabby looked away from her and shrugged. "I don't know what to believe anymore."

"Well, this isn't entirely what I came here to discuss with you," Jenni started. "Perhaps you'll choose not to believe me about this, too."

Tabby shifted her gaze, her eyes softening slightly. "What?"

"I had a board meeting at the hotel on the corner of Fifth tonight, where I saw Drew. He wasn't alone."

Tabby's eyes narrowed in on her. "He was with another woman? They were doing something?"

Jenni nodded. "They were making out. I wanted you to know."

Tabby nodded. "Thanks." She walked to the door and opened it for Jenni. Jenni slowly moved to meet her at the door, not wanting to leave on such a low note.

"Tabby," Jenni began.

Tabby looked up, tears in her eyes. "I don't want to talk about it. Not tonight. And frankly…" Her words trailed off, and she looked away from Jenni.

"You'd rather not talk about it with me. Understood. And I'm sorry," Jenni mumbled. Without another word, she turned away and went to her car. If she looked over her shoulder, she wouldn't be able to leave. She could only imagine the pain coursing through Tabby's veins, and seeing that fixated on her face would have torn Jenni up inside. Tabby needed time to heal, and when she was ready to do that, Jenni would be there for her.

CHAPTER TWENTY-THREE

Tabby

T abby tapped her finger on the desk, staring blankly at the computer monitor. She leaned back in her chair and tried to focus on the words on the screen, but it was no use. After two days of trying not to think about Jenni, she found that her situation with her was the only thing she could think about.

She screwed up! Plain and simple. Get over her. But that was impossible. She was already losing complete control of her life, and with Drew off having sex with whomever he wanted and the kids spending more time with friends, she was left only with her thoughts, which all revolved around Jenni. What if she was being honest with her about having no recollection of signing that document? What if Tabby had pushed her away for no apparent reason?

More like plenty of reason. She didn't tell you that you were on the verge of losing your job. She knew and decided to leave you out of that.

While she didn't trust Jenni regarding matters pertaining to Capmed, Tabby did believe her about Drew. She had no reason to believe Jenni had made that up, especially since Jenni didn't know what hotel Drew was staying in. Her so-called husband was clearly not done messing around with other women.

The front desk phone rang, and she reached over and grabbed it. "Cardiology. This is Tabby."

"Thank goodness you answered." Hanna's rushed voice came on the phone. "I'm the only one here and the ER has been swamped. Any chance you can help a woman out?"

Tabby looked around the dead hallway. Working in the ER would be something that could clear her mind of Jenni; it was precisely what she needed. "Give me five minutes to let them know. I'll be right there."

"You're a blessing, Tabby. See you soon."

Tabby dropped the phone into the cradle and went to find the nursing manager. Three minutes later, she was heading down the elevator and straight to the ER. When the doors opened, she spotted the waiting room and sighed with relief. It was just the thing she needed. She picked up the pace, hurrying toward the front desk.

Hanna came out of a room and let out a relieved breath. "Thank heavens you're here. I've gotten some people into a room but haven't fully triaged them. The charts are there. If you could grab some and do the triage, that'd be great."

"I'm on it," Tabby replied. She grabbed the first file folder and walked over to a room. When she opened the door, she saw a young girl sitting on the bed. She was clutching her arm, and a woman knelt beside her.

"Hi, there. My name is Tabby, and I'll be one of the nurses taking care of you. What happened here?" She grabbed a stool and wheeled it over to the bed, glad to finally be able to clear her mind of all her problems.

For the next hour, Hanna and Tabby worked simultaneously on assisting patients. It gradually became a well-oiled machine, and they kept it going. Tabby grabbed another folder and looked at the room number. She headed down the hallway, spotting Hanna as she rounded the corner. Hanna no longer looked stressed, and she was smiling again.

"Couldn't have done this without you, Tabby."

Tabby nodded. She always felt a sense of belonging when it came to Capmed. It was something she would surely miss if she did find herself terminated. She knocked on the next door. A voice sounded on the other end, which she took as an invitation to enter.

"Hello, I'm Tabby and I'll be your..." Her voice dropped when she saw Jenni sitting on the bed. "Jenni!" Tabby exclaimed. "I didn't notice it was you."

She looked at the chart, and sure enough, Jenni's name was in bold lettering. She felt foolish for having missed that small detail. "Is everything all right?" She sat down on the stool and let out a small, embarrassed laugh. "Well, of course everything isn't all right. You're here."

She opened the folder and looked at the main reason Jenni was there. She frowned, her brows furrowed. "The drugs aren't working?" she asked. "Looks like you've been throwing up for twenty-four hours and your migraine is at a twelve on a scale of ten."

Jenni looked down at the floor. "I'm feeling much better," she said in a small voice. "I shouldn't bother you. Just thought Hanna would be my nurse."

"Sorry to disappoint you," Tabby muttered.

"It's me disappointing you—that you have to be stuck taking care of me. Maybe I should have gone to another hospital."

Her eyes darted to Tabby's, but then she winced and fell back against her pillow. Tabby stared at her. It appeared that even sitting up for two minutes was too long for Jenni. "Lean back," Tabby ordered.

Jenni rolled her eyes and reclined in a more comfortable position. Tabby helped her lie back, positioning a pillow behind her head. "Thank you," Jenni said.

With the way Jenni was looking at her, Tabby felt weak herself. She turned away and moved back to her stool, then slowly sat down. "So, twenty-four hours, huh?"

"Give or take," Jenni replied. She closed her eyes and Tabby looked down at the file.

"The medicine was working," Tabby said.

"It probably still is, but I've been busy and haven't been able to take it regularly." She shrugged. "Gotta do what you gotta do."

"At the expense of your health?" Tabby asked, arching an eyebrow. Jenni opened her eyes and looked over to where Tabby sat. "Doesn't seem smart, if you ask me."

Jenni sighed. "I didn't miss the drugs on purpose. I've just been busy and ultimately just forgot. They warned me that this could happen if I missed two consecutive doses. They weren't wrong." She sat up, then clutched her head and slowly lay back down. "I just need some anti-nausea pills and then I promise I won't be missing any more of my medication."

"I would advise you not to," Tabby replied. She stood to get the thermometer and took Jenni's temperature. "One hundred point three." She tilted her head. "You have a fever, you're visibly shaking, and you're as pale as a sheet."

"Must be a wonderful sight," Jenni said. Her sarcasm wasn't very effective since the pain in her head was so strong, she had to speak in a whisper.

"I'm not saying that to be cruel. Just pointing out the obvious. Maybe you have more than just a reaction to not taking the medicine."

Jenni shook her head, then grimaced. "I would say it's just a reaction. I know my body is putting up a fight because I haven't been kind to it. That's all."

"All right then," Tabby softly stated. She grabbed the BP cuff and put her stethoscope in her ears. As she pumped the cuff up, she spotted Jenni watching her.

"Tabby," Jenni whispered.

"Shhhh," Tabby ordered. "I have to concentrate." She looked back down at what she was doing, but Jenni's eyes didn't sway from her, though Jenni didn't attempt to interrupt her again.

"BP is a little high," Tabby said. "Does it usually run high?" Jenni shook her head as Tabby documented the information. "Could be part of it, as well." She walked over to the door, then looked over her shoulder at Jenni. "I'll grab a doctor. They'll be in with you soon."

Before Tabby could leave, Jenni spoke up. "Are we going to talk about it?" she asked.

Tabby sighed. "I'm not sure we have anything to say to each other."

"I don't think that's true," Jenni quietly replied. "I know that I have a ton I want to say."

Tabby shrugged. "Just concentrate on getting better. The doc will be right in with you."

She left the room and closed the door before falling back against it. She didn't like seeing Jenni in pain, but dwelling over what she couldn't change wasn't going to do anything. She needed distance.

She dropped the file into the bin attached to the door and stood there for a moment, wondering if she should go back in to tell Jenni that all was going to be well. Instead, she headed back to the front desk for the next patient. She didn't know if all would be okay, but she knew that she had taken steps to ensure she was in a better position.

❈❈❈❈❈❈❈

Tabby slipped her phone back into her pocket as she left the breakroom and headed to the elevator. As she rounded the corner, she spotted two employees by the bulletin board. She hesitated before she proceeded to the elevator. "What's going on?" she asked.

A woman turned to Tabby. She had only seen her around

a few times, but she knew she worked in the basement, where the archived medical records were.

"They just put up a sign-up sheet for the upcoming fundraiser." Noticing Tabby's frown, the woman continued, "You know, the fundraiser?"

Tabby looked confused. "I haven't heard about it, but I have been pretty busy." Life and work had been hard to balance, especially with her marriage in shambles and her trying not to think about losing her income. "What is it?"

The other woman, a newer employee, at least according to the tag on her name badge, said, "They're having a fundraiser to save the staff. Look."

Tabby looked at the sign. "Save the Staff—catchy name."

The younger woman laughed. "Either way, I'm excited to help out in any way I can. I might not be one of the ones in jeopardy, but you just never know when you might need help."

Tabby nodded and looked at the signatures that were already present. Jenni's name was the first on the list, and her contact information was listed. "Jennifer Jennison is in charge?" she asked.

"Appears that way," the older woman, named Hazel, responded. "She not only donates money, but pitches in when needed."

"Looks like it," Tabby said. She picked up the pen attached to the list and signed her name on one of the few spots left. The fundraiser might be part of the reason Jenni was too busy to remember to take her medicine. It wasn't an excuse to ignore her health, but it was a sign that Jenni wasn't on board when it came to letting the employees go. The two women left, and Tabby pulled her phone from her pocket.

She hadn't heard from Jenni since she had assisted her in the ER two days earlier, and she had considered texting her to see how she felt, but had always stopped herself. If she reached out, that would mean that she was ready to forgive Jenni completely. She hadn't been ready, but she knew now that she was wrong in the way she had been treating Jenni.

She dialed her number, but it went straight to voicemail. "You've reached Jenni. Leave me a message and I'll call you back. Have a blessed day."

"Hey, Jenni. It's me. I know you're probably going to be surprised to hear from me, and I don't blame you. If the positions were reversed, I would be, too. Anyway, I was hoping we could talk. I saw the volunteer sign—or, at least, one of them. And..."

She paused, then continued. "Well, we'll discuss it when we can see each other. I work for another two hours and then I have a small errand I have to take care of. The kids are staying at friends' houses tonight, so I have the whole night free. If you have some time, maybe we can chat. Maybe I can swing by your place. Let me know. I'll be waiting for your call. Goodbye, Jenni. Oh, and I hope you're feeling much better." She hung up and got on the elevator to return to the cardiology floor.

It was a busy night, so Tabby found herself lost in work and not thinking about what she would say to Jenni. After her shift, she changed into everyday clothes and left with her purse in hand. She was hopeful that she'd be able to talk to Jenni, except Jenni hadn't called her back, and that made her feel strange. Maybe Jenni wasn't going to easily forgive her because Tabby hadn't believed her about the staff cuts.

Tabby drove with purpose, to make the one stop she knew

she had to make that night—the hotel where Drew was staying. With the kids away from the house, she would use that time to have a real conversation with Drew; she was ready to make that happen.

She approached the front desk, determined to get to his room, tell him why she was there, then leave. The quicker she could get through it, the easier the departure would be.

"May I help you?" a young petite blonde asked.

"I need the room number of Drew Brickly," she replied, confidence oozing from her tone.

The woman looked down at her computer and nodded. Without hesitation, she swiveled in her chair and grabbed a room key, then handed it over to her.

Tabby frowned. "I'll just knock." She pushed the key away, and the woman frowned.

"The way it works is you go in and…" Her words trailed off, and she lowered her voice. "Make yourself comfortable."

Tabby's jaw fell open. Without questioning the receptionist, she grabbed the key from the woman's hand and looked down at the number. "Thank you," she mumbled.

Tabby didn't waste any time getting on the elevator and taking it two floors up. Make herself comfortable? Was that what the staff was used to saying? She tapped her foot nervously, in tune with the music that played over the speaker in the elevator. When the doors opened, she walked to Drew's room. She stood, looking at the room key before taking a deep breath to steel herself.

Tabby swiped the key and opened the door. The first thing she was struck with was the darkness of the room. Perhaps Drew wasn't in. She moved in farther and heard the sound of running water. He was there. She hesitated, fearful of what she would discover in the bathroom. Or worse, in the shower.

A woman moaned, followed by the sound of something hard hitting up against a wall. Tabby shook her head and moved forward. "Drew!" the woman cried. That sound set something off inside of Tabby. She wanted to see Drew and the woman face to face.

Tabby threw the door back, and the woman—a brunette —along with Drew, abruptly stopped and turned to face her. The woman's eyes were round, her mouth wide open.

"Tabby!" Drew exclaimed.

Tabby shook her head. "There's not a single word you could say to me that would make this okay. And everything I want to say to you would make me look *very* unladylike. You don't deserve for me to even speak to you. You'll be hearing from my lawyer."

She spun on her heel and didn't shed a single tear. She ignored Drew, who was calling out for her. She was done with him, and there wasn't anything that her soon-to-be ex-husband could say to change that.

When she got to her car, she collapsed against the back of the seat, a feeling of relief washing over her. She was grateful that she was getting out of a dangerous situation—dangerous to her heart, anyway. Her phone rang, and she grabbed it before it could go to voicemail. Jenni's name flashed like bold letters, beckoning her to where she needed to be.

"Hello?"

"I'm sorry I'm just now calling you. My phone battery was dead, and I just got your message."

"I need to see you. Are you free?" Tabby asked.

"Come on over," Jenni said. Tabby put the car in drive and headed the short distance to Jenni's, knowing full well that when she saw her there would be no stopping the way her body and heart would react. She was finally right where she was supposed to be and hopeful that Jenni felt the same way.

CHAPTER TWENTY-FOUR

Jenni

Jenni paced in front of her bedroom mirror, then turned back to her reflection. She untucked her shirt from her jeans and tilted her head. "My goodness, Jenni, you're acting like a lovestruck teenager." She groaned and grabbed a hair tie, then pulled her hair into a loose ponytail. At least now she didn't appear like she cared how she looked.

Tabby rang the doorbell, and she jumped. She had wondered why Tabby had suddenly changed her mind. Was it just because she saw the posters calling for volunteers? She hadn't considered that might be the thing that would make Tabby reach out. At least the posters showed Tabby that Jenni was trying to help Capmed's staff, not get them fired.

Jenni left her room and hurried down the stairs, only slowing when she was close to the door. She had already mentally prepared herself that nothing was going to happen, but it didn't mean she couldn't look cute while Tabby was gently letting her down.

She opened the door to see Tabby turned away, looking out at the street. Her eyes darted to Jenni's. "Hey," Tabby said softly.

"Hey."

Tabby moved in closer, and for the first time in a while, she smiled. It was ever-so-slight, but it was there. It brought renewed hope to Jenni's mind.

"How are you feeling?" Tabby asked.

"Much better. I took my medicine, as planned, and I'm no longer nauseous." Jenni leaned against the door opening, realizing Tabby was still standing on her porch. "Silly me. Come inside." She stepped back, opening the door wider for Tabby to come into the foyer.

When Jenni closed the door and turned back around, Tabby swooped in for a kiss. Her hands softly but firmly grasped Jenni's face, knocking the wind out of Jenni. "Tabby," Jenni breathlessly gasped.

Tabby pulled back, her eyes now steady on Jenni's lips. "I couldn't wait to do that. I'm sorry, Jenni. I'm sorry I didn't believe you about the hospital. I'm sorry that I turned my back on you. The truth is that from the moment I got to know you, I started falling for you. It was scary, but also one of the best feelings in the world. Knowing that I was married caused me shame, but I don't regret these feelings I have. What I do regret is looking for a reason to push you away."

She shook her head. "No more. Now I'm only looking for

a reason to stay in your arms. I hope that you can accept my apology."

"I already have," Jenni said, wrapping her arms around Tabby and pulling her into a passionate and lingering kiss. "I already have," she whispered again before her lips crashed back onto Tabby's and their tongues collided wildly. She grabbed onto the base of Tabby's shirt and pulled her as they maneuvered back to the stairs.

As they walked up, their mouths still glued to each other, Jenni stumbled, which brought them both to a fit of giggles. They ran up the stairs, not stopping until they reached Jenni's bedroom. Tabby grabbed for the tie to Jenni's ponytail and quickly tugged on it, releasing Jenni's hair around her shoulders. Tabby pushed Jenni toward the bed, and together, they fell onto her pillowtop mattress and started pulling at each other's clothes until they were all shed and lying in a heap.

"I've been falling for you from the moment I first saw you," Jenni whispered between kisses. "That very moment." Her tongue swooped in, claiming a moan from Tabby.

Jenni reached up and slowly started to tweak Tabby's nipples between her fingers, eliciting some of the most pleasurable sounds Jenni had ever heard. Tabby maneuvered her body until she straddled Jenni, leaving Jenni breathless and gasping for air. She tossed her head back, groaning and just letting Tabby pleasure her as she wished.

Was she dreaming? It almost felt like she was, and she didn't want anything to wake her up. With her eyes closed, she allowed Tabby's soft lips to do as they pleased.

She grabbed handfuls of Tabby's hair between her fingers and didn't shift her body beneath her. She was getting everything she desired and more. There wasn't any fear that Tabby would rush out on her and go back to her husband. There weren't any thoughts that Tabby wasn't right where she wanted to be. There were only the two of them, and it felt so good.

<hr/>

Jenni pulled herself up and looked at Tabby, who had a content smile on her lips. "Did that just happen?" Jenni asked.

Tabby nodded, grinning from ear to ear. "Not once, but twice. Give me a minute and I'll be ready for a third round." Tabby brushed her lips against Jenni's, still smiling. "Who knew love could feel so amazing?"

Jenni laughed. "Who knew how much I would love hearing you call it love." She kissed Tabby harder and brushed her hand over Tabby's face. "Who knew how much I was truly falling for you over the time I was getting to know you?"

"I think I hoped." Tabby smiled. She sighed happily and fell back, the covers dipping lower to reveal her right breast. Jenni looked down at the perky nipple and she groaned, biting back the desire to move back in and claim another taste. Who knew a new love could be so exciting?

"What I didn't know," Tabby began, like she read Jenni's thoughts, "was that I would come here and immediately jump in bed with you. I didn't know a conversation I needed to have with Drew would end with me catching him and his mistress together in the shower."

Jenni sat up, her jaw dropping. "You what?" Jenni asked.

Tabby nodded. "I went to the hotel he's staying in. When

I asked for his room number, the receptionist simply handed over a key and told me to just go on in. Who's to say how many trysts he's had since we've been separated, or even before? But I can tell you this—no more. I'm done. I'm not going to find myself in a situation like that ever again." Tabby shivered, her eyes moving over to the bedroom window with a faraway look. "He played me like a fiddle repeatedly, and I allowed him to do that. How stupid could I be?"

"Don't say that," Jenni murmured. "You're not a fool. He's a jerk, and he never deserved you. But something good came out of your union. Two good things, in fact. You have two beautiful children together. They know the light you are in their lives. So, don't worry about your husband."

"Soon to be ex-husband," Tabby asserted.

"Have you started the paperwork?" Jenni asked, hope lifting her voice.

"I called my lawyer on my way to you, and she's drawing up divorce papers as we speak. Well, it's kind of late, so probably tomorrow." She laughed. Her whole face lit up, and Jenni couldn't remember seeing Tabby look so happy. Even after the first night they had sex, she seemed to be struggling. This was a good sign, Jenni believed.

"I'm truly happy for you," Jenni said, kissing Tabby, then pulling back and moving down to take her nipple into her mouth. She sighed with pleasure, releasing it from her lips to look up at Tabby. "It was just waiting for me."

Tabby laughed. "Couldn't help yourself, right?"

Jenni smiled deviously. "Not hardly." She kissed Tabby's shoulder, overwhelmingly in love with the way she felt around

Tabby. Every look sent shivers of desire through her, and Jenni was ready to shout from a rooftop how much she cared for her.

"So did you sign up to volunteer for the fundraiser?" Jenni asked, changing the subject.

"What do you think?" Tabby asked, arching an eyebrow.

"I would hope yes, because it wouldn't be the same without you." Jenni brushed a kiss on Tabby's forehead before pulling back. "I'm famished. Aren't you?"

"Sex does make a person need food," Tabby replied in jest. "Let's eat."

They both left the room, neither concerned with putting clothes back on. The night had started in a way that sent pleasurable shivers down Jenni's spine, and they were both looking for a more intense and erotic night than they'd ever spent together.

Jenni grabbed two glasses, a carton of milk, and a pie out of the refrigerator and started setting up the table. When she sat, she saw that Tabby was no longer smiling, but biting her lip nervously.

"What's wrong?" Jenni asked.

"Do you think you'll be able to save our jobs?" Tabby asked.

Jenni nodded and looked at her lover reassuringly. "Honestly, I believe that with the donors we've already gotten, everyone's job is safe."

EPILOGUE

Tabby

Three months Later

T abby looked across the room as Jenni spoke to a group of donors. She was laughing and working the crowd. She couldn't believe Jenni was doing this all for her. Well, her and the rest of the staff at Capmed. And, if given the opportunity, she had the perfect way to thank her. Unfortunately, Jenni kept being pulled in a thousand different directions by donors and staff alike.

A man cleared his throat, and Tabby looked over at him. "Mr. Chandler," she said.

"You've worked at Capmed long enough. I think it's safe to start calling me Brian."

Brian had a wide grin on his face. He always seemed to be more of a business type with a bite that matched his bark, but tonight, there was something different about him. He held a pleasant smile and his aura seemed to light up the rest of the room. "She did amazing work, don't you think?"

"Jenni? The best," Tabby replied. "Now hopefully it works." She said the latter part in an undertone, hoping he hadn't heard her, but when he shot her a knowing glance and chuckled, she knew she had been caught.

"I can assure you that it did. I have never seen this much money coming in in all my years in charge at the hospital. At the end of the night, I'll be announcing that no staff will be losing their jobs and it's all thanks to Jenni."

She smiled and nodded. "Thank you, Mr.—I mean, Brian." He patted her on the shoulder.

"Enjoy the rest of the night," he said, walking away.

Tabby beamed as she watched the crowd, reflecting on her journey. The past three months had been a long road. Her divorce had been finalized just two days before the fundraiser. She never thought she would see that day. What brought her solace and love was Jenni. She had stayed by her side every single day, making sure Tabby felt that she was loved, and didn't let Drew's negativity pull her down. While he was still the girls' father and she was prepared to co-parent with him, they couldn't be married. And she was relieved that her children didn't seem to mind the change of events.

Tabby looked across the room, where Brittany was reading a story to a toddler, showing her the illustrations, and not looking like she minded being there. Callie was in the midst of many kids, playing blocks with them, laughing and having a good time. They wanted to be there and knew that Jenni made her happy. It was the only thing that they cared about.

Tabby turned back to Jenni, who just happened to look toward her. They shared a sweet and intimate look, one that stayed hidden from everyone else. The only people aware of their relationship were Callie and Brittany. Tabby and Jenni had felt it was best so no one could judge them, knowing Tabby wasn't divorced. Now that the divorce was final, who cared what anyone thought?

Tabby proceeded through the crowd and headed up to the makeshift stage in front of everyone, where a microphone stood, waiting for someone to take the floor. She tapped on the microphone and a squeal sounded, causing all heads to turn her way.

"Sorry about that," she said. A few people laughed around her, and she continued. "I want to thank you all for coming out and doing your part to save the staffing over at Capmed. I, for one, could never repay you and appreciate all that everyone has done. But I also know that none of this would have been possible without one person. And I would like to call her up here now. Jennifer Jennison, will you please come take the stage?"

Jenni's cheeks were red as she came onto the stage. Her eyes locked on Tabby's. "You're embarrassing me," she whispered, then laughed lightly.

Tabby smiled broadly. "Those who know Jenni know that she doesn't like the limelight. She did all of this without expecting so much as a thank you. But for anyone who knows me, you know that I couldn't allow tonight to end without expressing my gratitude to her. So, thank you, Jenni. From the bottom of my heart, I appreciate you."

Jenni nodded. "You're welcome. Now, are we done here?"

She started to leave, but Tabby reached out and took her hand.

"Not so fast." She kept her fingers laced between Jenni's. "What most people here don't know is that I have had the privilege of getting to know this woman, through good times and bad, sad times and sorrow, and, well, the list goes on. There were so many obstacles I've had to face in these past months, and I couldn't have faced them without this woman."

She turned her attention to Jenni. "Jenni, you are my light. You are my sunshine. And you are the woman that I know destiny has brought into my life, because I needed someone that would be there to protect me. I needed someone to love me and my children like no one else could."

Tabby smiled wider when she saw the loving look that Jenni sent her way. "I thank God every day for bringing you into my life. And I want the whole hospital—the whole world, even—to know that Jenni Jennison and I are officially a couple."

The crowd erupted into applause, and before Jenni could stop Tabby, Tabby leaned in and kissed her. Jenni pressed her hand to Tabby's chest, then fully let go and succumbed to the moment. They kissed on the stage as everyone applauded and cheered around them.

"I love you," Tabby whispered, pulling back.

Jenni looked at Tabby tenderly. "I love you."

With their hands still locked, they got off the stage, and Jenni pulled Tabby behind the stage, pressing her firmly against the wall. Jenni kissed her with a passionate hunger, and Tabby succumbed to those feelings right there in the back of the convention center. Jenni was the woman Tabby knew she would spend the rest of her life getting to know and falling deeper in love with. And one day, marriage would come. But for now, she was just happy living in the moment and excited for the love between them to flourish. She was getting her happily-ever-after fairytale after all.

MT CASSEN BOOKS

Available In Paperback, Ebook, And Audio Formats. Click Here:
https://mybook.to/MELODYINHERHEART

Available In Paperback, Ebook, And Audio Formats. Click Here:
https://mybook.to/FIGHTINGHERTOUCH

Available In Paperback, Ebook, And Audio Formats. Click Here:
https://mybook.to/PROTECTINGHERHEART

Available In Paperback, Ebook, And Audio Formats. Click Here:
https://mybook.to/TOOLITTLETOOLATE

YOU CAN HELP OTHERS!

A big thank you for trusting my book with your time, attention, and support. Here are three points to remember about reader comments (aka book reviews):

1. I read all reader comments so I can fix any errors and make my next book even better. "***Get busy polishing or get busy rusting***," is my motto as a writer. I believe that good books are brought forth consistently when an author's persistence is enabled by the generous expressions of reader intent as seen in reviews and purchases.
2. Most readers read the reviews to help guide their purchases. I don't buy anything before looking at the reviews. Your reviews help readers.
3. Now, you're all ready to drop a comment, but analysis paralysis gets the better of you. You might think: *What would I even write about? Who's going to read*

my review, anyway? You might also think: ***What if Crazy Uncle Bob were to see my review?*** Then, after a few minutes of panicking, you would probably think: *Wait, why is Crazy Uncle Bob* ***secretly reading lesbian romance novels****?*

So, please snap out of your analysis paralysis. I have added here some questions on which other readers would want your opinions: a) How would you have handled Tabby's dilemma? b) What kind of impression did Jenny make on you? c) What would you like to communicate to other readers who may be interested in this book? Think of these questions as kick-starters for your review. Please drop your honest opinions here:

https://www.amazon.com/review/create-review?ASIN=
B09LTW47VP
or click on the QR Code below:

That would make my day! Thank you!

Please subscribe to my newsletter and grab a free book here:
https://BookHip.com/KWQLLMN

Happy Reading,
Morgan

P.S: Thanks, www.kindlepreneur.com, for the QR code generator and www.booklinker.com for the universal links.

ABOUT THE AUTHOR

Morgan Cassen

WITH ROXIE

Morgan Cassen writes Lesbian Romance. Her mission is to make the world safer for sapphic stories to be told. Yes, she knows that there are millions of romance writers and billions of romance novels. So, why would she even think of adding to the pile? Well, Morgan has seen enough to know that the truly interesting stories are not what happen between human beings. That gig can seem pretty tame. At least compared to its older, tempestuous sister. Let's bring out Ms. Inner Conflict, the queen of all drama in the human world -- the ruler of the emotional map. Yes, the conflict between everything you've worked for and everything you want. You never imagined that all your hard work would put you so far away from everything you wanted. Also, how about the conflict between the past and the future? Being true to the past would require you to keep the future so far away in the future. But, how long can you postpone the future? What if your whole framing of the past can't stand the scrutiny of thoughtful analysis today even as you resolutely push the future away? Huh, what do you do with that kind of conflict? The conflict between human beings can look so tame compared to the real thing: conflict between you and you. You are the hero and villain at the same time, but the problem is that the villain thinks she is the hero, while the hero is all caught up in doubt. Which you will you choose? No, nobody else will make that choice for you. You get to make that choice, and your comforting, trusty friend--procrastination--can't seem to do the trick this time. The time has come for you to choose. See, inner conflict is where it's at. Inner conflict is what Morgan writes about in her books. Please join her as she writes the stories of breakup and love that tug at heartstrings.

Morgan is indebted to Sarah Wu (copyeditor) and Dr. Peter Palmieri and Nurse Karen Stockdale (medical advisors) for their extraordinary work and diligence. This book is so much better because of their efforts.

Stalk the author using the link below:

www.mtcassen.com

ABOUT PETER PALMIERI
(MEDICAL ADVISOR)

Peter Palmieri, M.D., M.B.A. is a licensed physician with over 20 years of practice experience in Chicago, Dallas, Houston, and the Rio Grande Valley in Texas. He received his B.A. from the University of California San Diego, with a double major in Animal Physiology and Psychology. He earned his medical  degree from Loyola University Stritch School of Medicine and a Healthcare M.B.A. from The George Washington University. He is a regular contributor of original articles to a variety of health and wellness blogs.

ABOUT KAREN STOCKDALE
(MEDICAL ADVISOR)

Karen Stockdale, MBA, BSN, RN is an experienced nurse in the fields of cardiology and medical/surgical nursing. She has also worked as a nurse manager, hospital quality and safety administrator, and quality consultant. She obtained her ASN-RN in 2003 and her BSN in 2012 from Southwest Baptist University. Karen completed an MBA in Healthcare Management in 2017. She currently writes for several healthcare and tech blogs and whitepapers, as well as developing continuing education courses for nurses.

Karen's websites are:
https://www.linkedin.com/in/karen-stockdale-5aab2584/
and
http://writemedical.net/

ABOUT SARAH WU
(COPYEDITOR)

Sarah was born and raised in the concrete jungle of NYC. She loves traveling, exploring different foods, and giving the occasional tree a big hug. When Sarah isn't polishing up manuscripts, she enjoys spending time with loved ones and lovingly but firmly heckling them to decrease their plastic consumption.

Printed in Great Britain
by Amazon

37588702R00138